"Insidiou[...]
reviles as w[...]
Wri[...] ————————————————— [...]ievement Award

"Without Fu-Manchu we wouldn't have Dr. No, Doctor Doom or Dr. Evil. Sax Rohmer created the first truly great evil mastermind. Devious, inventive, complex, and fascinating. These novels inspired a century of great thrillers!"—Jonathan Maberry, *New York Times* bestselling author of *Assassin's Code* and *Patient Zero*

"The true king of the pulp mystery is Sax Rohmer—and the shining ruby in his crown is without a doubt his Fu-Manchu stories."—James Rollins, *New York Times* bestselling author of *The Devil Colony*

"Fu-Manchu remains the definitive diabolical mastermind of the 20th Century. Though the arch-villain is 'the Yellow Peril incarnate,' Rohmer shows an interest in other cultures and allows his protagonist a complex set of motivations and a code of honor which often make him seem a better man than his Western antagonists. At their best, these books are very superior pulp fiction... at their worst, they're still gruesomely readable."
—Kim Newman, award-winning author of *Anno Dracula*

"Sax Rohmer is one of the great thriller writers of all time! Rohmer created in Fu-Manchu the model for the super-villains of James Bond, and his hero Nayland Smith and Dr. Petrie are worthy stand-ins for Holmes and Watson... though Fu-Manchu makes Professor Moriarty seem an under-achiever."—Max Allan Collins, *New York Times* bestselling author of *The Road to Perdition*

"I grew up reading Sax Rohmer's Fu-Manchu novels, in cheap paperback editions with appropriately lurid covers. They completely entranced me with their vision of a world constantly simmering with intrigue and wildly overheated ambitions. Even without all the exotic detail supplied by Rohmer's imagination, I knew full well that world wasn't the same as the one I lived in... For that alone, I'm grateful for all the hours I spent chasing around with Nayland Smith and his stalwart associates, though really my heart was always on their intimidating opponent's side."
—K. W. Jeter, acclaimed author of *Infernal Devices*

EMPEROR
FU-MANCHU

THE COMPLETE FU-MANCHU SERIES
BY SAX ROHMER

Available now from Titan Books:
THE MYSTERY OF DR. FU-MANCHU
THE RETURN OF DR. FU-MANCHU
THE HAND OF FU-MANCHU
THE DAUGHTER OF FU-MANCHU
THE MASK OF FU-MANCHU
THE BRIDE OF FU-MANCHU
THE TRAIL OF FU-MANCHU
PRESIDENT OF FU-MANCHU
THE DRUMS OF FU-MANCHU
THE ISLAND OF FU-MANCHU
THE SHADOW OF FU-MANCHU
RE-ENTER: FU-MANCHU

Coming soon from Titan Books:
THE WRATH OF FU-MANCHU

EMPEROR
FU-MANCHU

SAX ROHMER

TITAN BOOKS

EMPEROR FU-MANCHU
Print edition ISBN: 9780857686152
E-book edition ISBN: 9780857686817

Published by Titan Books
A division of Titan Publishing Group Ltd
144 Southwark Street, London SE1 0UP

First published as a novel in the UK by Herbert Jenkins, 1959
First published as a novel in the US by Fawcett Gold Medal, 1959

First Titan Books edition: September 2015
10 9 8 7 6 5 4 3 2 1

The Authors League of America and the Society of Authors assert the moral right
to be identified as the author of this work.

Visit our website: www.titanbooks.com

Did you enjoy this book? We love to hear from our readers.
Please email us at readerfeedback@titanemail.com or write
to us at Reader Feedback at the above address.

To receive advance information, news, competitions, and exclusive offers online,
please sign up for the Titan newsletter on our website: www.titanbooks.com

Frontispiece illustration from the *Emperor Fu-Manchu* first edition paperback
cover, Herbert Jenkins, 1959.

A CIP catalogue record for this title is available from the British Library.

Printed and bound in the United States.

Cover illustration from the British first edition hardcover of
Emperor Fu Manchu, published in 1959 by Herbert Jenkins.

CHAPTER ONE

"Once you pass the second Bamboo Curtain, McKay, unless my theories are all haywire, you'll be up against the greatest scientific criminal genius who has ever threatened the world."

Tony McKay met the fixed regard of cold gray eyes which seemed to be sizing him up from the soles of his shoes to the crown of his head. The terse words and rapid, clipped sentences of the remarkable man he had come to meet penetrated his brain with a bulletlike force. He knocked ash from his cigarette. The sounds and cries of a busy Chinese street reached him through an open window.

"I didn't expect to be going to a cocktail party, Sir Denis."

Sir Denis Nayland Smith smiled, and the lean, tanned face, the keen eyes, momentarily became those of a boy.

"I think you're the fellow I'm looking for. You served with distinction in the United States Army, and come to me highly recommended. May I ask if you have some personal animus against the Communist regime in China?"

"You may. I have. They brought about my father's death and ruined our business."

Nayland Smith relighted his briar pipe. "An excellent incentive. But it's my duty to warn you about the kind of job you're taking on. Right from the moment you leave this office you're on your own. You're an undercover agent—a man alone. Neither London nor Washington knows you. But we shall be in constant touch. You'll be helping to save the world from slavery."

Tony nodded; stabbed out his cigarette in an ashtray. "No man could be better equipped for what you have to do. You were born here, and you speak the language fluently. With your facial features you can pass for Chinese. There's no Iron Curtain here. But there are two Bamboo Curtains. The first has plenty of holes in it; the second so far has proved impenetrable. Oddly enough, it isn't in the Peiping area, but up near the Tibetan frontier. We have to know the identity of the big man it conceals. He's the real power behind the strange scheme."

"But he must come out sometimes," Tony protested.

"He does. He moves about like a shadow. All we can learn about him is that he's known and feared as 'the Master.' His base seems to be somewhere in the province of Szechuan—and this province is behind the second Bamboo Curtain."

"Is that where you want me to go, Sir Denis?"

"It is. You could get there through Burma—"

"I could get a long way from right here, with a British passport, as a representative of, say, Vickers. Then I could disappear and become a Chinese coolie from Hong Kong—that's safe for me—looking for a lost relative or girl friend, or somebody."

"Make your own choice, McKay. I have a shrewd idea about the identity of the Master."

"You think you know who he is?"

"I think he is the president of the most dangerous secret society in the world, the Si-Fan—Dr. Fu-Manchu."

"Dr. Fu-Manchu."

"I believe he's up to his old game, running with the hare and hunting with the hounds—"

There was a sound resembling the note of a tiny bell. Nayland Smith checked his words and adjusted what looked like an Air Force wrist watch. Raising his hand, he began to speak into it. Tony realized that it must be some kind of walkie-talkie. The conversation was unintelligible, but when it ended, Nayland Smith glanced at him in an odd way.

"One of my contacts in Szechuan," he explained drily. "Reports the appearance of another Cold Man in Chia-Ting. They're creating a panic."

"A Cold Man? I don't understand."

"Nor do I. But it'll be one of your jobs to find out. They are almost certainly monstrosities created by Dr. Fu-Manchu. I know his methods. They seem to be Burmese or Tibetans. Orders are issued that anyone meeting a Cold Man must instantly report to the police; that on no account must the creature be *touched*."

"Why?"

"I can't say. But they *have* been touched—and although they're walking about, their bodies are said to be icily cold."

"Good God! *Zombies*—living dead men!"

"And they always appear in or near Chia-Ting. You should head for there. You'll have one of these." Nayland Smith tapped the instrument he wore on his wrist. "I may as well confess it's a device we pinched from Dr. Fu-Manchu. Found on a prisoner. It looks like a wrist watch. One of our research men broke down the formula and now a number of our agents are provided with them. You can call me here at any time, and I can call you. Whatever happens, don't lose it. Notify me regularly where you are—if

11

anything goes wrong, get rid of it, fast."

"I'm all set to start."

"There's some number one top secret being hidden in Szechuan. Military Intelligence thinks it's a Soviet project. I believe it's a Fu-Manchu project. He may be playing the Soviets at their own game. Dr. Fu-Manchu has no more use for Communism than I have for Asiatic flu. But so far all attempts to solve the puzzle have come apart. Local agents are only of limited use, but you may find them helpful and they'll be looking out for you. You'll have the sign and countersigns. Dine with me tonight and I'll give you a thorough briefing."

CHAPTER TWO

There was a rat watching him. In the failing light he couldn't see its body, but he could see its eyes. Waiting hungrily, no doubt, for any scrap of rice he might leave in the bowl. Well, the rat would be in luck. The rice was moldy.

Tony McKay drank a little more tepid water and then lay back on his lice-ridden mattress, his head against the wall, looking up at a small square window. Iron bars crisscrossed the opening and now, as dusk fell, hardly any light came in. He could have dealt with the iron bars, in time, but the window was just out of reach—two inches out of reach.

It was another example of Chinese ingenuity, like the platter of ripe peaches his jailer had left in the dungeon one morning. By walking to the end of the chain clamped to his right ankle and lying flat, he could stretch his arm across the grimy floor—to within two inches of the fruit!

But none of their cunning tricks would pay off. Physically he was getting below par, but his will remained as strong as on the day he left Hong Kong, unless...

He dismissed the thought.

A dark shape crossed the pattern of the bars, became lost in the shadow of a stone ledge which ran from the window around the angle to the grilled door. Two more wicked little eyes appeared beside the pair in the corner of the cell. The rat's mate had joined up.

He didn't mind them. In their repulsive way, they formed a sort of link with the free world outside.

He fell into a sort of dozing reverie. These reveries had saved his sanity, given him the strength to carry on.

It was hard to grasp the fact that only two weeks ago he had been in Hong Kong. Throughout the first week he had kept in close touch with Nayland Smith, and this awful sense of loneliness which weighed him down now had not swept over him. Once he had overcome his stage fright over assuming the role of Chi Foh, a Hong Kong fisherman, he had begun to enjoy his mission…

There were faint movements in the corridor, but they ceased, and Tony returned again to the recent past which now seemed so distant…

Anyway, he had penetrated the second Bamboo Curtain—was still behind it. Of the mystery brain which Sir Denis Nayland Smith believed to be that of the fabulous Dr. Fu-Manchu, he had learned less than nothing. But in one part of his mission he had succeeded. The discovery had been made because of the thoroughness with which he had taken over the assumed identity of a Hong Kong fisherman seeking a missing fiancée. He had selected a remote riverside village not far above Chia-Ting on the Ya Ho River as the place to which his mythical girl friend had been taken by her family.

Quite openly he canvassed the inhabitants, so that if questioned later he could call witnesses to support his story. And it was from a kindly old woman that he got the clue which led him to his goal.

She suggested that the missing girl might be employed in "the

Russian camp." It appeared that a granddaughter of hers had worked there for a time.

"Where is this camp?" he asked.

It was on the outskirts of the village.

"What are Russians doing there?" he wanted to know.

They were employed to guard the leprosy research centre. Even stray dogs who came too close to the enclosure were shot to avoid spreading infection. The research centre was a mile outside the village.

"When did your granddaughter leave, and why?" he inquired.

To get married, the old woman told him. She left only a month ago. The wages were good and the work light. She and her husband now lived in the village.

Tony interviewed the girl, describing "Nan Cho," his missing fiancée, but was assured that she was not employed at the Russian camp. He gathered that there were not more than forty men there in charge of a junior officer and two sergeants.

How vividly he remembered his reconnaissance in the gray dawn next morning.

The camp was a mere group of huts, with a cookhouse and an orderly room displaying the hammer and sickle flag. He estimated that even by Russian standards it couldn't accommodate more than forty men. From his cover he studied it awhile, and when the sleeping camp came to life decided that it was the most slovenly outfit he had ever come across. The entire lack of discipline convinced him that the officer in charge must be a throw-out, sent to this dismal post because he was useless elsewhere.

There was a new and badly made road leading from the camp up into the hills which overlooked the river. He was still watching when a squad of seven men appeared high up the road, not in any kind of order but just trudging along as they pleased. The conclusion was obvious. The guard on the research centre had been relieved.

He made a wide detour. There was plenty of cover on both sides of the road, oaks and scrub, and not a patch of cultivation that he could see. It was a toilsome journey, for he was afraid to take to the winding road even when far out of sight of the camp below. This was fortunate, for suddenly, beyond another bend of the serpentine road, he came in sight of the research station.

It was unlike anything he had anticipated.

A ten-foot wire fence surrounded an area of some twelve acres. Roughly in the centre of the area, which had been mowed clear of vegetation and looked like a huge sheet of brown paper, he saw a group of buildings roofed with corrugated iron.

The road ended before a gate in the wire fence. There was a wooden hut beside the gate, and a Russian soldier stood there, his rifle resting against the hut. He was smoking a cigarette.

Presently another man appeared walking briskly along outside the wire. The smoker carefully stubbed out his cigarette, stuck it behind his ear, and shouldered his rifle. The other man stepped into the hut. Evidently, he was the corporal in charge who had posted the remaining five men in his squad at points around the fence.

The cunning of Soviet propaganda! Leprosy is a frightening word, although leprosy had rarely appeared in Szechuan. But the mere name was enough to keep all at a distance.

This was the germ factory.

Where had he gone wrong?

Chung Wah-Su? Was it possible that Chung had betrayed him? It would be in line with Chinese thinking (if he, Tony, had aroused suspicion) to plant a pretended helper in his path. Yet all that Chung Wah-Su had done was to admit that he worked for Free China and to give him directions how best to cross the Yangtze into

Szechuan without meeting with frontier guards.

It was hard to believe.

There was the man he knew simply as Li. Who was Li? True, Tony hadn't trusted him very far although he had given sign and countersign, but all the same it was Li who had put him in touch with Chung Wah-Su.

Had Li been seized, forced to speak? Or was it possible that a report of Tony's visit to Hua-Tzu had preceded him down the river? Questioned, he had spoken freely about the visit; for although he knew, now, what was hidden there, he couldn't go back on his original plan without destroying the carefully planned evidence of the purpose of his long journey.

He fell into an uneasy doze. He could hear and smell the rats in his rice bowl. As he slipped into sleep, his mind carried him back to his last examination by the dreadful creature called Colonel Soong...

"If you searched this village you speak of, looking for some girl, you can tell me the name of the former mandarin who lives in the big house."

"There is no large house in Hua-Tzu."

"I mean the house in the hills."

"I saw no house in the hills."

His heart warmed again in his near-dream state. There were few Americans, or Europeans either, who could have sustained the character of a lovelorn fisherman from Hong Kong under the fire of those oblique, ferocious eyes.

Yes, Sir Denis Nayland Smith was a good picker. No man could be better fitted for the job than one born in China, one whose maternal grandmother had belonged to an old Manchurian family.

* * *

In a small room, otherwise plainly furnished, a man sat in a massive, high-backed ebony chair behind a lacquer desk. The desk glistened in the light of a silk shaded lantern which hung from the ceiling in such a way that the golden dragons, designed on the lacquer panels, seemed to stir mysteriously.

The man seated there wore a loose yellow robe. His elbows rested on the desk, and his fingers—long, yellow fingers—were pressed together; he might have reminded an observer of a praying mantis. He had the high brow of a philosopher and features suggesting great intellectual power. This aura of mental force seemed to be projected by his eyes, which were of a singular green color. As he stared before him as if at some distant vision, from time to time his eyes filmed over in an extraordinary manner.

The room, in which there lingered a faint, sickly smell of opium, was completely silent.

This silence was scarcely disturbed when a screen door opened and an old Chinese came in on slippered feet. His face, in which small, twinkling eyes looked out from an incredible map of wrinkles, was that of a man battered in a long life of action, but still unbowed, undaunted. He wore an embroidered robe and a black cap topped by a coral bead.

He dropped down onto cushions heaped on the rugs, tucking his hands into the loose sleeves of his robe, and remained there, still as a painted Buddha, watching the other man.

The silence was suddenly and harshly broken by the voice of the dreamer at the lacquer desk. It was a strange voice, stressing the many sibilants in the Chinese language and emphasizing the gutturals.

"And so, Tsung-Chao, I am back again in China—a fugitive from the West, but a power in the East. You, my old friend, are restored to favor. General Huan Tsung-Chao, a former officer of the Chinese

Empire, now Communist governor of a province! A triumph for the Si-Fan. But similar phenomena have appeared in Soviet Russia. You have converted Szechuan into a fortress in which I am secure. You have done well."

"Praise from the Master warms my old heart."

"It is a stout heart, and not so old as mine."

"All that I have done has been under your direction."

"What of the reorganization of the People's Army? You are too modest, Tsung-Chao. But between us we have gained the confidence of Peiping. I have unlimited authority, for Peiping remains curiously, but fortunately, ignorant of the power of the Si-Fan."

"I pray that their ignorance may continue."

"I have inspected many provinces and have found our work progressing well. I detected several United States agents, and many from Free China. But Free China fights for the same goal as the Si-Fan."

"But not for the same leader, Master!"

Dr. Fu-Manchu smiled. His smile was more terrifying than his frown.

"You mean for the same *Emperor!* We must be patient." His voice rose in exaltation. "I shall restore this ancient Empire to more than its former glory! Communism, with its vulgarity, its glorification of the worker, I shall sweep from the earth! What Buonaparte did, I shall do, and as he did, I shall win control of the West as well as of the East!"

"I await the day, Master!"

"It will come. But if the United States, Britain, or especially Soviet Russia, should unmask the worldwide conspiracy of the Si-Fan, all our plans would be laid in ashes! So, when I am in China, my China, I must travel incognito; I must be a shadow."

The old general gave a wrinkled and humorous smile. "I can answer for most of our friends in Formosa. From the United States agents you have little to fear. None of them know you by sight, only by name. I have entertained several Soviet visitors and your name stands high with the Kremlin. But news reached me yesterday that Nayland Smith has left England, and I believe he is in Hong Kong."

"Tehee!" It was a hiss. "The old hound is hot on my trail. He will not be working alone. We must take precautions. He lacks genius. He is a product of the Scotland Yard tradition. But he has inexhaustible patience. Heed this, Tsung-Chao: any suspect arrested by the blundering Communists in or near Szechuan must be reported to me at once. I shall interrogate such suspects personally."

Tony awoke with a start, and shot upright in bed.

It wasn't the rats or the lice. It was a woman's scream that had pierced his sleep like a hot blade.

Everything was silent again, the night hot and still. His cell stank foully. But he knew he had not dreamt it. He had heard a woman's scream—a sudden, agonized scream. He clenched his fists and found that his palms were clammy. And he listened—listened.

He had no means of knowing what time it was or how long he had slept. The barred window resembled a black hole in the wall. It overlooked a small courtyard and he could barely see the sky.

Further sleep was out of the question. His brain was on fire. Somewhere, in this hell hole, they were tormenting a woman.

Footsteps and voices broke the silence. He recognized one voice, that of his jailer.

They were coming for him! This would be the great test.

The heavy door was unlocked. Two armed men wearing the

uniform of the Red Army held up lanterns. His thickset, leering jailer opened the padlock which confined McKay's ankle.

"This way, Chi Foh. They want to ask you something about fishing!"

He assumed that air of stony passivity which belonged to his role. Head held low, he went out between the two guards. Quite unnecessarily, they prodded him with their rifle butts to keep him moving. Strange how Soviet training dehumanized men.

Colonel Soong sat at a bamboo table in the lighted courtyard. The governor, an older man, sat on the colonel's right. A junior officer, who looked like a coolie in uniform, was on his left. Two soldiers stood behind them.

"Stand him there," Colonel Soong commanded, pointing, "where he can see what we do with spies!"

The governor had put on thick-rimmed spectacles and was trying to read some document which lay before him—probably the several examinations of Suspect Wu Chi Foh. The junior officer watched Tony with the kind of expression a gourmet might have when beholding a choice meal.

"Those who admit their guilt, Chi Foh," the colonel was saying, "die an easy death. I recommend an open confession. Bring in the prisoners."

Escorted by four soldiers, two men came into the courtyard, their hands tied behind their backs.

Tony saw the elderly Chung Wah-Su and the younger Li. He had covered many hundreds of miles by road, river and canal since his dealings with them. Yet here they were to confront him, lined up no more than three paces away.

"Wu Chi Foh, do you know these men? Make them look up."

Guards prodded the prisoners. Both stared impassively at Tony.

"No, Excellency."

"You are a lying son of a pig! Again I ask you—and this is your last chance for an easy death—do you know these men?"

"No, Excellency."

Colonel Soong fired a harsh order. The official executioner came in, a stocky, muscular figure stripped to the waist and showing a torso and arms like a gorilla's. He carried a short, curved sword.

Neither of the prisoners displayed the slightest interest in the proceedings.

After, with an efficiency that stunned Tony, Chung Wah-Su and Li had been beheaded and their bodies hauled from the courtyard, Colonel Soong told him, "That is the easy death, Chi Foh. I am returning you to your cell to consider. Be prepared at any hour to find the same painless end."

Tony was dragged back to the smelly dungeon which had confined him for so long and was thrown in with such sudden violence that he fell on his face. The chain was relocked to his ankle.

He dropped onto the bed and held his head in his hands.

Even supposing that neither Chung Wah-Su nor Li had involved him in their confessions (and it was possible), he was marked for death. He could admit what little he had learned and have his head neatly lopped off by an expert, or he could persist in his story that he was a harmless fisherman. Then he would be put in the stocks, and—

They had no evidence whatever to connect him with Sir Denis Nayland Smith. The wonderful little long-range walkie-talkie which Sir Denis had entrusted to him before he set out, he had, mercifully, managed to drop in the river when he saw them coming to arrest him.

He seemed to hear again that snappy voice. "If anything goes wrong, get rid of it, fast." It had helped him in many emergencies, made him feel that he wasn't alone. Now…

He could, of course, reveal his true identity and challenge Soong to execute a United States officer. But even that probably wouldn't stop the colonel.

This was the end.

Something came through the window bars and fell right at his feet.

It made a dull thud, but there was a faint metallic jingle, too. Tony stooped eagerly and picked up a piece of thin paper wrapped around two keys and another metal object.

His hands shook as he unrolled the parcel. The third object was a cigarette-lighter.

He snapped up the thin rice paper and read:

From Nayland Smith.
The smaller key frees your chain. The other opens the door. Leave before daylight. The guard on the gate is bribed. Your boat still lies where you left it. Money and some food aboard. Follow Min River left bank, down to any navigable creek, then use irrigation canals to Niu-fo-tu on Lu Ho River. Ask for the house of the Lama. He expects you. Memorize and swallow message.

His heart leapt madly. Thank God! Nayland Smith hadn't lost contact with him. His last message on the walkie-talkie had placed his location, and he was no longer alone.

Tony had little difficulty in memorizing the directions, for his journey up to Chia-Ting had made him familiar with the river and villages. He swallowed the piece of rice paper, then had to make a lightning decision about the keys. Footsteps sounded in the passage. Voices. They were coming back for him.

He thrust the keys and the lighter under his mattress.

But in his heart he knew help had come too late.

"Colonel Soong is asking for you, fisherman!"

His leering jailer threw open the cell door. Two men, the same ones as before, stood by while the chain was unfastened, then banged his ribs with their rifle butts as he was marched along the passage and out again into the courtyard.

Many men have been condemned for cowardice in the face of the enemy. But knowing what was in store for him, Tony wondered if Nayland Smith would understand if he simply accepted "the easy death" and became another missing agent. For he couldn't hope to survive the ordeal ahead.

If he could, and did, stay silent, and they released him, which was unlikely, his sufferings would have rendered him useless, helpless; his memory gone. He would be a mere shell of a man.

"Have you anything more to say, Chi Foh?"

"No, Excellency."

Tony was forced onto his knees in front of the stocks, facing outward, and his feet were clamped in the openings provided. Then, wrists piniuned behind, his body was drawn as far back as it would go without something snapping, and the rope was tied to a crossbeam.

The executioner, satisfied, awaited orders.

"For the last time, Wu Chi Foh, have you anything to say?"

"Nothing, Excellency."

Colonel Soong raised his hand.

"Release the prisoner!"

Colonel Soong's hand remained raised. It was held in a viselike grip by a Nubian of enormous stature. The ebony giant had rested his free hand on the shoulder of the Chinese lieutenant, who was clearly unable to stir.

"I gave an order."

The mist was dispersing more and more. Now, half in the shadow of an archway behind the table, Tony could see a tall figure. The executioner was electrified. In a matter of seconds Tony found himself free and saw the executioner bowing humbly to the man who stood motionless in the archway.

Another crisp command, not spoken in Chinese, resulted in the Nubian's stepping back. Both officers sprang to their feet, spun around and stood at the salute.

"Colonel Soong," the imperious tones carried clearly all over the courtyard, "it is contrary to my wishes that these primitive methods of questioning be employed. China will flower again as a land of beauty and culture. If harsh means must be used to extract the truth, at least let them be refined. Brutality without purpose is neither successful nor artistic. Remain in your quarters until I send for you."

Colonel Soong retired, followed by his lieutenant.

"I will interview the prisoner."

CHAPTER THREE

Tony, dazed, bewildered, and with the numb calm of utter desperation, found himself in an elaborately furnished room, most likely the prison governor's study. He was facing a long desk, overly ornamented in the Burmese manner, behind which was a commodious chair. He was tinglingly conscious of the giant Nubian at his elbow.

No one else was there until the man who had ordered his release entered.

He came in from the other end of the room and walked to the desk. His movements had a catlike quality; his step was feline, silent. Tony could not mistake the tall, lean figure which he had glimpsed in the courtyard. He recognized the sort of cavalry cloak in which the man with the imperious voice had been wrapped and which he now discarded and dropped on the rug beside the chair.

Tony saw that he wore a uniform resembling those worn by Prussian officers. He had glossy top boots. As he took his seat, resting his elbows on the desk and pressing his long, yellow fingertips together, Tony experienced a fluttering in the stomach.

He was looking at one of the most fascinating faces he had ever seen. The high forehead, the chiseled, aggressive nose, the thin lips, were those of an aristocrat, a thinker and a devil. But the long, half-closed eyes of an astonishingly green color completed the impression of force which radiated from this man's personality, as he sat there, perfectly still.

Suddenly he spoke.

"Well, my friend, I think the time has come for you to lay your cards on the table. Don't you agree with me?"

The last shadow of doubt was swept from Tony's mind. He recalled fragments of Nayland Smith's vivid word picture of the person he was seeking. "A brow like Shakespeare and a face like Satan. Eyes of the true cat-green. He speaks every civilized language with near perfection, and knows countless dialects as well. He has the brains of any three men of genius."

Tony found it impossible to sustain the stare of those hypnotic eyes. But he knew that here was Number One, the Master.

This was Dr. Fu-Manchu!

The shock of hearing the question in perfect English was so unexpected that he nearly betrayed himself by replying in the same language.

It was a crucial test. And he survived it.

"I don't understand, Excellency," he said in Chinese.

"Don't be a fool. You understand well enough."

Tony shook his head in a bewildered way. Meeting the intolerable stare of those green eyes, he was aware that, again, his life hung on a thread.

Silence. The Negro behind him made no sound. He could hear the faint spluttering of perfume sticks set before a shrine at one end, of the room. The air was oppressive. He was becoming dizzy. His appalling experience and imprisonment had stolen his stamina.

He was brought back by a brusque question in Chinese.

"Your name is Wu Chi Foh? You are accused of spying?"

He met the hypnotic stare.

"Yes, Excellency."

In that fleeting second he had discovered something. The disturbing element in Fu-Manchu's gaze was that he seemed to be looking not at him, but through him.

"Are you guilty?"

"No, Excellency."

"For a humble fisherman, you have a pure accent. You interest me. Take him back to his cell."

For once, Tony was glad to throw himself wearily on the filthy mattress, glad even to find brief sanctuary in his dungeon from those dreadful eyes.

"Leave before daylight…"

He jumped up, stared at the barred window. He could see the stars against a gray background. Dawn was breaking.

"Your boat still lies where you left it…"

But had the arrival, clearly unexpected, of the Master, put the scheme out of gear? Had the guard on the gate been changed? Was the sampan still lying in the river?

The key of the leg chain worked rather stiffly and gave him some uneasy moments. But at last a welcome click came and his leg was free. His heart pounded hard as he fitted the second key into the keyhole of the door. It turned without a hitch. He swung the heavy door open and looked out cautiously into the stone-paved passage.

There was no one there. Only a very faint light came through a barred window at the end. He heard nothing and slipped out into the cool, open air.

He clung close to the buildings in the deserted courtyard. A shadow of the whipping post lay like a band across the stone paving. No window showed any light. At last he got to the corridor which led to freedom. He peeped around an angle of the wall. The prison had been a fortress in feudal times and just inside the great nail-studded gate there was a cramped guardroom.

A dim light, probably that of a lantern, shone out from the guardroom door.

And he had to pass that door.

He inhaled deeply, then moved ahead. He saw no one inside. The lantern stood on a table. He passed, and came to the gate.

The bolts which seemed to be well oiled were already withdrawn from the sockets which secured the gate.

Inch by inch, Tony swung open the mass of teak and iron. When the gap was wide enough to slip through, he stepped out, paused for a moment, breathing hard, then gently reclosed the gate.

He set off at a good pace, but avoided running. His escape had been perfectly planned. The guard had only to shoot the bolts into place, employ his national talent for lying, and the prisoner's disappearance would look like magic, for Tony had taken the keys and the lighter with him. Flawless teamwork. It must have cost a lot of money.

When he came to the river, there was his old sampan, tied up to a rickety stage.

Not pausing to examine the craft, he cast loose the mooring line and stepped onto the oarsman's platform, aft.

When day broke he was many miles south. He tied up in a cactus-lined backwater from which he could see no sign of a nearby road. Then he stooped under the strip of plaited roof, and went in to find where the money was hidden and what provisions he had.

There was a Chinese girl asleep in the cabin.

* * *

She was curled up on a heap of matting, one arm half covering her face. Her clothes were at least as ragged and soiled as his own and her black hair was disheveled. He could see that she had long dark lashes, and there were tear tracks from her closed eyes cutting through the dirt on her cheeks.

How had she got on board, and when?

Anyway, here she was, and he had to decide what to do with her. An added problem, when he had far too many to cope with already. But there was nothing he could do about her now, while she was still sleeping.

Creeping quietly out to the stern, carrying soap and shaving material, he stripped, soaped himself all over, and then dropped into the cool water. Climbing back, much refreshed, he toweled and, stifling his disgust, got into the filthy rags which were all he had. Then he lighted his galley fire—an iron bucket with holes punched in it—using dry wood gathered on the bank, and boiled a pannikin of water.

He was struggling through his first shave in more than two weeks when he saw the girl watching him. He paused, shaving brush in hand, and stared. He had expected coal-black eyes but her eyes were dark blue. He remembered that some of the up-country peasants had blue eyes. She looked like a very dirty Chinese doll. "So you are awake at last?"

"Yes." She looked down and shuddered. "How long did I sleep?" She had a pretty, bell-like voice, but it shook nervously.

"I don't know." More to reassure her than for any other reason he went on shaving. "When did you come on board?"

"Some time last night," she answered.

Wiping his face, he began anxiously to forage in the locker. His own few pots and pans were there. He had jettisoned everything incriminating when he realized they were coming to arrest him. He found a considerable sum of money, mostly in small currency, and there were cigarettes and a carton of canned meat, soup, and other edibles. He also discovered some sea toast, rice, fresh fruit, soap, shaving kit, matches, a bottle of lime juice, and a bottle of Scotch. And, last of all, a .38 and a box of shells.

Then, resoaping his chin, he went on shaving again. "You came on board at Chia-Ting?"

"Yes. Please don't throw me off. I don't know what I shall do if you won't let me stay."

At Chia-Ting. The ways of these people were strange and tortuous. Did they know more than he supposed? Was this little stowaway a spy? Perhaps it was a plot to learn where he was going, to identify his associates.

He finished shaving. The girl, her hands clasped, waited with pleading eyes.

"What's your name?"

"Yueh Hua. I can cook, and fish, and manage a boat. I won't be any trouble."

Yueh Hua meant "Moon Flower." This poor little waif hardly looked the part.

"Where did you come from?"

"A small village ten miles from Chia-Ting. It is called Su-Chien."

"And what were you doing in Chia-Ting?"

"Running away from my stepfather." She spoke eagerly. "He had sold me to Fuen Chang, a horrible old man who would have beaten me. It is his only pleasure, beating girls."

"You had friends in Chia-Ting, I suppose?"

"Yes." Yueh Hua nodded. "My sister. But she had gone. There was nothing to do but try to get to my aunt. It is a long way."

Tony sponged his face, washed the shaving brush, and began, very thoughtfully, to clean the razor blade. If this girl was an agent of the Master she certainly knew her piece.

"Where does your aunt live?"

"In Lung Chang."

"Where is Lung Chang?"

"On the Lu Ho."

This startled him. He was far from sure of his route to the Lu Ho.

"Do you know the way to Lung Chang?"

"Of course!" There was a flash of white teeth in the grimy face. "I used to go there in my father's boat. I mean, my real father."

"I see." He replaced the razor in its box. "What I don't understand is why you came onto my boat and fell asleep."

"I was tired and frightened. I had walked a long way. People were beginning to notice me—to follow me. I came on your boat to hide, I don't remember falling asleep. Are you angry with me?"

CHAPTER FOUR

Some hours before this conversation took place, a less amiable conversation had been held in the office of the governor of the prison. Dr. Fu-Manchu sat behind the desk. The old governor and Colonel Soong stood before him.

"I fear, Colonel Soong, that we have here some serious breach of discipline. There would seem to be traitors among your men." He spoke softly, but there was menace in every syllable.

Colonel Soong's voice was unsteady when he replied. "I assure you, Most High, it is not so. This man's escape was magic."

The narrowed green eyes were turned in the old governor's direction.

"Who had charge of the keys?"

"The head jailer, Highness."

"Where are they now?"

"In their usual place where he put them after having relocked the prisoner in his cell after his interview with Highness."

"Were they ever left unprotected?"

"Never. The head jailer and another were in the room up to the

33

very moment that Highness ordered the prisoner to be brought here again."

"Unless both men are lying, duplicate keys were smuggled into the prisoner's cell. And what of the main gate?"

Colonel Soong broke in. "The main gate was found locked, Most High. The man on guard reports that no one passed, that the gate was never opened."

Dr. Fu-Manchu took a pinch of snuff from a small silver box before him. "I shall interrogate these men later. I have means of learning the truth without resorting to your barbarous methods, Colonel Soong. The discipline of your men is disgraceful. Several patients undergoing special treatment in the clinic which I recently established have wandered from the compound and into the town. Yet you have orders to patrol the area day and night. These patients are suffering from a dangerous infectious disease. How do you explain this laxity?"

Colonel Soong's yellow face had assumed a gray tinge. "Most High, my troops have orders not to touch them, although some have done so. They report that these people are not human. They say they are dead men who have escaped from their tombs."

"Fools!" Dr. Fu-Manchu's cold voice rose on a sudden note of frenzy. "I am doomed to be served by fools." He clenched his hands, and by an obvious effort of will conquered his anger. "This man who calls himself Wu Chi Foh must be recaptured. You lost him. Find him. Colonel Soong, move! I shall accompany you."

Tony decided that his best course was to pretend to believe Yueh Hua so he asked, "Is Lung Chang far from Niu-fo-tu?"

"About eight miles. We have to pass it. We used to come to this place sometimes, too. It is called Pool of Lily Dreams. Once it was part of the garden of a big house. But the house has gone. May I come and show you the way to Niu-fo-tu? I can row the boat when you want to rest."

Her eagerness was pathetic. He nodded, and smiled for the first time.

"All right, Yueh Hua. I'll take you to Lung Chang."

"Oh, thank you! You are very good." He read deep gratitude in her blue eyes. "Please," she said as he was about to replace his washing kit, "may I—"

Tony handed her the soap and the comb. "The towel's wet, but it's the only one."

Yueh Hua grabbed them and jumped ashore. He saw her heading for a clump of alders where the bank sloped down to the pool.

He was hunting for some plausible explanation of how he had come by his canned provisions, when he heard her running back. Her hair was wet. And she was trying to fasten a ragged pajama jacket, which, with baggy trousers, made up her costume.

"Quick! We must be quick!"

She jumped on board with the agility of a wild goat, throwing down soap and towel.

"What's the matter, Yueh Hua?"

"Coming along—now! A motor boat. It must be the police—for *me!* They think I stole your sampan."

The widely opened eyes never wavered.

"Wait," Tony said. "Don't stir until I come back."

Yueh Hua was right.

An old fourteen-foot motor craft was coming down. Colonel Soong stood up in the stern, sweeping the banks on either side through field glasses.

Tony raced back. When he reached the boat he pulled up and

stared. Yueh Hua had cast off and stood at the oar, ready to leave.

"Be quick! I know a hiding place. These people are new here. They may not find us."

He climbed aboard and sat down watching her. He might as well let her have her way, for he had no plan of his own.

She swung the sampan about with an easy, deep sweep of the long oar. Then, using a minimum of effort, she headed straight across the pool, avoiding traps set by clumps of wild lilies, and drove straight through a forest of rushes with a sudden powerful stroke. For a moment, he thought they were stranded. Then, using the oar like a punt pole, Yueh Hua got the boat free, and they were in a smaller pool, deep and clear, roofed over by the foliage of majestic old willows.

"That was very good, Yueh Hua."

"Did you see who it was?"

"Yes. An Army officer, with field glasses."

"Not—a tall, thin man, wearing a long cloak?"

Tony was startled, but hid the fact. "No. Short, wearing a uniform. Are you afraid of this tall man?"

"Yes... *Ssh!* Sounds carry over the pool. They had stopped, but they are just turning in."

As she spoke the engine coughed into action again. Although he couldn't see, Tony knew that the motor boat had entered the narrow opening and that Colonel Soong would be inspecting the banks of the pool. They lay down side by side, peering through the rushes.

A sudden protective impulse made him put his arm around Yueh Hua's shoulders. She was trembling.

At last they heard Colonel Soong's grating voice. "Nobody here. Back out."

The motor craft went coughing out astern.

As the sound of the engine died away, Tony stood up, helping Yueh Hua to her feet. It was dark under the willows and he could hardly see her face.

"Thank you, Yueh Hua," he said softly. Then he ducked forward under the matting roof, turned his back, and lighted a cigarette.

His first ideas about Yueh Hua required an overhaul. Even Chinese duplicity couldn't account for what had happened. She was as scared of Colonel Soong as he was himself—and desperately afraid of Dr. Fu-Manchu. Her explanation that she might be suspected of stealing his boat didn't add up, either. Agreed that she was running away—but from *whom* was she running? Someone far more formidable than her stepfather.

He returned to the stern of the boat. Yueh Hua had washed and tidied up considerably. She was smiling shyly.

"Do I look any better?"

He thought she looked very well indeed. There were few Mongolian characteristics. Prominent cheekbones and very slightly slanting eyes, yes. But many Celts had these. Now that her face was clean, he saw that she had a fresh, healthy complexion. In fact, he decided that Yueh Hua was quite pretty in a quaint way.

He planned to remain hidden where they were until the searchers returned and passed on the way up to Chia-Ting. Yueh Hua shook her head.

"When they don't find the sampan anywhere we could have gotten to in this time, they will search again on the way back. Someone may tell them of this place. It was once used as a duck decoy."

Tony thought of his .38 and wondered how many of the crew, beginning with Colonel Soong, he could knock off as they came into the decoy. But he dismissed the idea quickly.

"We shall have to cross the river before they come back, and hide

37

in a creek I know there," she continued.

"Is it used much?"

"No. It is too shallow."

This idea was a desperate venture. Should the motor cruiser turn about sooner than anticipated, they could be trapped on the way over. He pointed out that Soong might search the creek.

"It is upstream. They will have searched it coming down."

Tony grasped the long sweep and began to pole along the bank, edging the boat toward the opening through the rushes.

"Nearer the middle," Yueh Hua directed. "Look—where the dragonfly is."

He gave a powerful thrust. The bow of the sampan was driven in about three feet, then progress was checked.

"Another push from this side, hard."

He swung the oar over, found a firm spot, and thrust with all his weight. The boat glided along an unseen channel, and they were out again in the main part of the pool.

"Let me go ashore first and see if the river is clear," Yueh Hua said.

Tony rowed in to the spot against which he had first tied up, and she leaped ashore lightly and ran off through the cactus lining the bank. He waited, listening. And as he listened, he heard voices singing some monotonous song, and discerned the faint sound of a reed pipe.

Yueh Hua came running back.

"A big raft coming down! They may have been told to look out for us. We must wait until they pass."

He nodded. But every minute's delay might mean capture.

The sounds drew nearer. The song was a bawdy thing once popular on the Hong Kong Flower Boats. Tony glanced at Yueh Hua, but read only anxiety in her face. They stayed quite silent until the raft had gone by.

Then he swung the sampan through the opening. The stream was deserted. Piloted by Yueh Hua, they crossed. Tony found the narrow creek and rowed the boat into it until Yueh Hua called, "Stop here."

There was a rough hut under the trees. He turned to her in sudden doubt.

"Are there people here?"

"I hope not. It is used sometimes by fishers, but nobody lives in it."

In fact, the tumble-down place proved to be deserted. It was so far decayed that not even an eel fisherman would have consented to live there. The palm roof was full of holes and the bamboo framework largely collapsed. When he had tied up the boat, he secretly charged his .38 and slipped its comforting weight into a pouch inside his ragged pants.

"I must find my way along the bank to the end of the creek, Yueh Hua, and watch for the motor boat."

She touched his arm. "Please, let me come, too."

They set out together in blazing sunshine. There was a sort of path through thick undergrowth, but evidently it hadn't been used for a long time. Then came the bare banks lower down. There was a wandering gully, though, which gave good cover and led them to the river only some yards above the creek.

They had trudged along in silence. Now both looked upstream. The raft was no longer in sight. The river appeared deserted. They sat down side by side among the rushes and wildgrass, watching a slow tide go whispering by. Tony felt that Yueh Hua was furtively studying him. He glanced at her.

She smiled. "What is your honorable name, if you please?"

"My family name is Wu. I am called Chi Foh."

"Mine is Kwee. You don't belong in this part of China?"

He looked at her searchingly. She was still smiling.

"No. My father—" He hesitated. He had nearly said "was a merchant."—"is a storekeeper in Hong Kong. I was brought up there."

"I suppose, Chi Foh, he was ruined by the war?"

But he didn't answer. He had heard the asthmatic coughing of Colonel Soong's motor craft. They were coming back, close to the right bank.

Yueh Hua grasped his hand. He saw that her lips trembled. "We must lie behind these rushes, Chi Foh. We can see from there, but they won't see us."

They crept back from the bank and lay down next to each other. The old cruiser was very close now.

Almost unconsciously, he put his left arm around Yueh Hua's shoulders.

From where he lay, he couldn't see Soong in the stern. But he could see a man who stood up in the bows. It was the giant Nubian.

Then he heard a clear, imperious voice. It sent a trickle of ice down Tony's spine.

"I fear, Colonel Soong, that you are wasting valuable time."

The motor boat had swung around slightly on the current. He saw Soong in the stern, field glasses in hand, and he saw someone else seated in the cabin behind the man at the wheel. A figure wrapped in a dark cloak.

Yueh Hua shuddered so violently that he glanced at her anxiously. Every trace of color had left her face.

"Don't be afraid," he whispered, and held her closely. "They can't see us."

But she didn't answer. Colonel Soong's harsh voice was raised unsteadily. "I assure you, Most High, it is not so. The escaped prisoner must certainly have come this way."

"I regret that I cannot share your confidence." The words were spoken in sibilant, cultured Chinese. Then in another language, which Tony thought might be Arabic, a short sentence followed.

The Nubian spun around and stood at attention. He shook his head and answered briefly in the same guttural tongue.

"I was inclined—" Fu-Manchu was addressing Soong—"to send Mahmud ashore again to search the hut on the creek. But he assures me no one has been there. I believe him, for he has the instincts of a hunting leopard." The motor cruiser had drifted now to within a few yards of the bank. It was plain enough that "Mahmud" on his former visit must have followed the gully in which they lay, that if he did come ashore again he could hardly fail to stumble over them.

Tony fingered the useful weapon in his pocket. The big Negro, if he came, might carry a gun. Soong was armed. There might be other arms on board. But there were only four men to deal with. Given luck, and surprise to help him, he thought he could deal with them.

Silence for a few seconds, and then, "Shall I go, myself, Highness?" Soong volunteered.

Tony was planning his tactics. If Soong came ashore, he would shoot the big Negro first, then, before the colonel could grasp what had happened, he would try for Soong.

"Proceed upstream," the imperious voice commanded. "We passed no other possible hiding place on our way down. Therefore, we cannot have left the sampan behind."

* * *

Late that evening, Dr. Fu-Manchu sat at the lacquered desk, reading. Old General Huan, from his favorite seat on cushions, watched him.

"I notice that André Skobolov is expected here tomorrow. You have instructions from Peiping to entertain him. Why was the presence of this dangerous Soviet agent in China not reported to me?" Fu-Manchu glanced up from the notes which lay before him on the desk. "It would seem that our intelligence service is sleeping."

General Huan Tsung-Chao shook his head slightly. "This man Skobolov travels almost as secretly as you do, Master."

Dr. Fu-Manchu's eyes glittered wickedly from under half-lowered lids. "I have perhaps been misled in my belief that the elusive escaped prisoner was a British agent acting under Nayland Smith. His remarkable disappearance is more easily explained if he is a secret agent of the Soviet. They have facilities here which are denied to Nayland Smith."

"If that were so, why should he have been imprisoned?"

"Wake up, Tsung-Chao. The identity of such an agent would not be known to the blundering Colonel Soong, nor to the prison governor. It pains me to think that I may have saved the life of a Soviet spy."

Old General Huan smiled a wry, wrinkled smile. "There is unfortunate news, Master, which may confirm your suspicions. But I am assured that Wu Chi Foh had no documents in his possession nor on his boat."

Fu-Manchu's eyes opened fully. They blazed. His expression remained immobile as a mask. But when he spoke his tone was very subdued, oddly sibilant.

"Unfortunate news? Documents? What have you to tell me?"

Outwardly calm, as always, Huan Tsung-Chao replied, "My house in Chungtu was entered last night and important papers stolen from my office. Among these documents—for no other valuables are missing—was the Si-Fan Register..."

Slowly, Dr. Fu-Manchu stood up. His hands were clenched. Yet, when he spoke again, his voice remained unemotional.

"The register is in the Si-Fan cipher, which has never been broken."

"*No* cipher is unbreakable, Master."

"Spare me your platitudes. But whether the register has been stolen by British or Soviet agents, it cannot be deciphered except by an expert, either in London or in Moscow. Was your safe forced?"

"The register was not in my safe. I kept it in what I believed to be a secret hiding place. Not even my steward, who sends me this bad news, knew of it."

"You mean," Fu-Manchu suggested softly, "that some supernatural agency has been at work?"

Huan Tsung-Chao maintained his phenomenal calm. "I mean that some spy armed with powerful binoculars has watched me through my study window, from a tree in my garden possibly, and has seen me open the receptacle. Entrance was made through this window by someone who silently climbed the vine outside."

Dr. Fu-Manchu slipped his hands into the loose sleeves of his robe and stared into space, standing perfectly still. There was a long, silent interval; then he spoke again.

"Why is Skobolov coming *here?*"

"Officially, as an attaché of the Soviet Embassy, to promote relations between Communist China and Soviet Russia. He wishes to meet prominent figures in the Chinese movement."

"But why *here* at your summer villa rather than at the official residence in Chungtu?"

"I frequently entertain here. It is more pleasant, except in winter."

"He is aware that I am here?"

Tsung-Chao smiled his wrinkled smile. "It is improbable since even I did not know of your arrival in China until you stood at my door."

Fu-Manchu remained as motionless as a statue. "He has courage. It was he, or a professional thief in his employ, who stole the register. While he is your guest he knows he is safe. We dare not make the attempt. But he will obey his orders and be here tomorrow. We cannot be sure that he has the register in his possession, but whether he has the register or is to meet the man who stole it, he is far too dangerous an enemy to be permitted to return to Moscow. For it is to the Kremlin he would report such a triumph, not to Peiping. André Skobolov must never reach Russia."

CHAPTER FIVE

Yueh Hua broke a long silence when she looked at Tony and asked, "Were you educated in Hong Kong, Chi Foh?"

"Yes. Why?"

"I knew you had more education than most fishermen. You are so kind to me."

"Aren't most fishermen kind?"

"Not the way you are."

Yes, he was hamming the part. He had shown her his small stock of un-Chinese provisions and told her that his father, the storekeeper, who knew he had acquired a taste for foreign delicacies, had packed a case for him when he left Hong Kong. She had laughed happily, clapped her hands. But he wondered if she had believed him. Except for the lime juice and the fresh fruit, she seemed to prefer the national monotonous rice. But she went for the cigarettes. All the same, Yueh Hua's keen feminine instincts might have detected some chink in the façade. He decided to shift the focus of interest.

"Yueh Hua, there's something I've been wanting to ask you." She lay very still. "Why are you so afraid of the tall man who wears a

45

long cloak, the man they call 'Most High'? Has he ever done you any harm?" Yueh Hua was so long in replying that he turned and looked at her.

"Shall I tell you, Chi Foh?" she asked softly.

"Of course. I want to know."

And as she stared up again at the broken roof of the mat-shed, he knew that she had been trying to make up her mind how far she could trust him, and that she had failed to reach a decision. He was sure that whatever she told him now wouldn't be the truth.

"Very well." She seemed to be thinking hard. "When I came away from the house where I thought I should find my sister, it was dark. I didn't know what to do or where to go. I had no money. I was afraid to speak to anyone. And there were soldiers in the streets. I was hiding from two of them in the shadow of a big gateway, when the gate was opened."

She stared fixedly up at the tattered palm roof.

"A tall man came out. He wore a uniform—an officer. Four men came out behind him. One was a black man, very big. He carried a lantern. The light shone on the officer's face and on his eyes, which were like pieces of green jade. You saw him in the boat. His eyes are like that."

"Yes, I suppose they are."

"I knew he could see me from where I was trying to hide. I turned to run. But I was too late. He called me back. You have heard his voice. No one would ever think of disobeying him. He was very gentle when he asked me some questions, but I was shaking so much I could hardly stand. He told me to wait inside the courtyard until he returned."

"And did you wait, Yueh Hua?"

"No. When the porter had locked the gate and gone inside the house I sat down on a bench and tried to think what to do. There was an old plum tree growing on one of the walls. It had very strong branches. I climbed up. Then I let myself drop on the other side. I tried twice to steal out of the town. But there were soldiers at both gates. Then I thought I would go down to the river and take a boat or try to swim across. Right at the end of the canal I found your sampan."

Tony considered this story with some care. It had at least one merit. It could be true. Yet he felt almost certain it wasn't.

"So you see," Yueh Hua said, "why I am afraid of him."

"Yes, of course." He tried to speak casually. "I suppose he is the Communist governor of the province?"

Yueh Hua shook her head. "No. I think he is something more than that. They treat him like the emperors used to be treated."

"Do you think he wanted you for himself?"

Yueh Hua shuddered visibly.

"I don't know, Chi Foh. But I should die if he even touched me."

Tony began to realize then, as they waited for sundown, that Yueh Hua knew the country well. This was another mark in her favor, for he knew less than nothing about it.

"What sort of place is Lung Chang, Yueh Hua?" he asked.

"A small town, Chi Foh."

"Your aunt lives there, you told me?"

"Yes."

"She is married, I suppose?"

"She is a widow. I shall be safe with her."

"Have you other friends there?"

"I expect they have all gone, those I knew. Everything is changed."

After careful consideration, he said, "Lung Chang has gone over to the Communists, I suppose, Yueh Hua?"

"Yes." She passed him a tin cup. "They all had to."

"You mean, they didn't want to?"

"No. Lung Chang for ever so long has been the property of the great Lao clan. The people all belonged to the estate. They were content. Now, they are miserable." Yueh Hua was watching him and smiling. It would be unwise to probe deeper, he decided.

"I have to see a man in Niu-fo-tu. Is it a small place, Yueh Hua?"

"Yes. But there is a market there. I think Niu-fo-tu is dangerous for us, Chi Foh."

And instinctively he knew she was thinking of the officer with eyes "like pieces of green jade."

They set out around sundown. By morning, Yueh Hua said, they would reach a canal which connected with a creek. It was rarely used and they could tie up there until it seemed safe to go on.

They sculled and rested in turn through the hours of the night. Sometimes, Tony would lean on the long oar and bend forward, looking in to see if Yueh Hua was asleep. At a place where the bank he followed became low, he swung in to a point made by several small creeks joining the river, which formed a little delta carpeted with wild hyacinths.

Yueh Hua woke up as the regular sweep of the oar stopped.

"Is anything the matter, Chi Foh?"

"No. I'm just thirsty," he said quickly. "Shall I make tea?"

"Not unless you want tea. Whiskey will do for me. Would you like some?"

"No, thank you. But I should like some lime juice." They sat and sipped their drinks, diluted with boiled water cooled in an old clay jar. This was a custom Tony followed throughout his journey. He used to do it in Burma and never had a trace of dysentery.

If Yueh Hua wondered about it, she never said so, and he knew that his use of chopsticks was faultless. Yet he often caught her watching him in a queer way.

He was sure of himself where passing acquaintances were concerned. But he hadn't counted on a close intimacy with any bred-in-the-bone Chinese. Almost hourly he found himself wondering if Yueh Hua suspected that he wasn't what he pretended to be.

It was a dim hour of the night, but old General Huan Tsung-Chao and Dr. Fu-Manchu still remained in conference in the room with the lacquered desk. Apparently, they had conferred there since dusk. Piles of documents littered the desk. General Huan, wearing horn-rimmed spectacles, was reading one of them. He glanced up, began to speak. Dr. Fu-Manchu, fingertips pressed together, sat with closed eyes and compressed lips.

"We can rely upon the armed forces in the four provinces adjoining Szechuan. Some seventy-five percent have joined the Si-Fan. I have a report here from Peiping which states that agents of Free China are securing many recruits, and I have ordered those of the agents who already belong to our Order to make sure of these recruits."

Fu-Manchu, still keeping his eyes closed, spoke softly. "There is a rapport between the free Chinese and the Secret Service of which our old friend, Nayland Smith, is an active member. Great caution is necessary. We are not ready. And if our present standing with Peiping should be disturbed—if they lost their confidence in me— our strategy would be badly shaken." His voice sank lower. "This loss of the register alarms me. Such evidence, in the hands of either the Allies or Russia, would destroy us."

"It is certain that the register could not be in the possession of the man called Wu Chi Foh and equally certain that he could not have stolen it. He was in prison at the time. I doubt if he is concerned in any way."

"Yet the affair, Tsung-Chao, was so cunningly contrived that some outside agency must have planned it. The escape was brilliantly managed and the complete disappearance of the man and his boat is phenomenal. Some hiding place had been prepared for him."

General Huan smiled wryly. "That is possible. But he may yet be found. It is now nearing the time when I must prepare to entertain André Skobolov."

"I have already made my preparations." Fu-Manchu's soft voice took on a sound that was more like a hiss. "I have some choice glossina in my laboratory, a highly successful culture. I shall take steps to ensure his mental incapacity and ultimate death. The symptoms will develop some hours after he leaves here. I selected this method as the most suitable. Mahmud and a selected party will cover his movements from the moment of his departure. They will take the first possible opportunity to seize any briefcase he may carry. If he has the register, we shall recover it, and if he has notified Moscow, his death, should the body be found, cannot be laid at your door. The trypanosomes which the insects will inject are so amplified that fatal conditions develop in twenty-four to thirty-six hours."

General Huan's wrinkled face assumed a troubled expression.

"I agree, although with reluctance, that this man's execution is necessary to our safety, but I do not understand how these insects to which you refer (I am a scientist only of war) are to be employed."

Dr. Fu-Manchu opened his eyes and smiled. It was a deathly smile. He dipped his long fingers in a silver snuffbox.

"I, also, have studied the science of war. But my strategy is designed to prevent it by removing those few who have power to loose upon the world forces of wholesale destruction. It is simple and it is just. I have ordered that one of my Cold Men be brought here. He will arrive about dawn. These living-dead, as the ignorant masses term them, are dispensable. And handling the glossina is very dangerous. I shall smoke awhile, Tsung-Chao, and repose, for I have much work to do. Be so good as to send Chung-Wa to prepare my pipe."

Dawn was stealing over the river when Yueh Hua piloted the sampan into the canal. They went up for a mile or more before coming to a place where a gnarled tree hung right over the water, forming a kind of green cover. They tied up under the tree.

It was as Tony was eating his unpalatable breakfast that a slight movement in a field of rape in full yellow bloom drew his attention to the bank. At first he thought he was mistaken. Then he knew he wasn't.

A pair of bright, beady black eyes peered out intently. Tony stood up, staring under raised hands. And presently, in rapid flight along a path through the five-foot high rape he saw a tiny boy, naked except for a loincloth. "Why should he run away, Yueh Hua?"

He saw her face flush.

"He may have been watching us for all sorts of reasons. I suppose he thought you would beat him."

An old rush basket, waterlogged and broken, was drifting toward them along the canal. He watched it until it reached the sampan. Then he pulled it on board.

"If anyone comes to ask questions, Yueh Hua, I shall disappear. Say this is your boat, and say that there has been no one else with you."

"As you wish, Chi Foh. But how are you going to disappear?"

A flight of wild ducks passed overhead. It was the fact that this marshy land teemed with wild fowl which had given him the idea...

"It may not be necessary. If it is, I'll show you."

While Yueh Hua washed the rice bowls, he made a sounding with the long sweep. He found more than five feet of water in the canal.

He had no sooner completed this than he saw that his disappearance was going to be necessary.

Far off across the fields, on the side to which they were tied up, a small figure, little more than a yellow dot in the distance, came running along an embankment. Two men in uniform followed.

"Yueh Hua!" He spoke quietly.

She turned. "Yes, Chi Foh?"

"Remember what we arranged. That little devil of a boy is bringing two soldiers. It's your word against his."

He ducked into the low cabin and came out carrying the pistol. Yueh Hua had seemed alarmed the first time she saw it, but now she smiled bravely and nodded her approval.

He managed to pull away the heavy iron pin which did duty as a rowlock and tied it to a line, on which he knotted a loop, and threw it overboard. Next, with a piece of string, he fastened the automatic around his neck. Then he went overboard himself, feet first, holding the ground line and the rush basket.

"Oh!" Yueh Hua's eyes danced joyously for one fleeting moment. "Like snaring wild duck."

He grinned cheerfully, although he felt far from cheerful, and hauled on the line until he could get one foot into the loop to steady him. Standing on the bed of the canal, he found that his shoulders were well above water. He waded several yards from the sampan, pulled the old rush basket over his head, and disappeared.

Through the basket's many holes he could see quite well. He unfastened his pistol and held it inside the basket clear of the water line.

If anything went wrong with Yueh Hua's story, he didn't mean to hesitate. There might have to be two casualties in the ranks of the People's Army.

The two men and the boy reached the canal bank. The boy was a grubby, little cross-eyed specimen. The men were shoddily dressed irregulars of the peasant type. They carried old service revolvers.

"We want to see the man, not you," one of them said.

He seemed to be the senior. The other, deeply pock-marked, stared dumbly at Yueh Hua.

"There's some mistake!" Yueh Hua stood upright, open-eyed. "There's no man on my boat!"

"You are a liar!" the boy piped shrilly.

Tony held his breath.

"And you're an ugly little son of a sow!" Yueh Hua screamed at him. "What lies have you been telling about me? I'm an honest girl. My mother is sick in Chia-Ting and I'm going to nurse her. If my father heard you, he would cut your tongue out!"

"Chia-Ting. Who is your father?" the man asked.

"My father is head jailer at the prison. Only wait until he hears about this."

This flight of fancy was sheer genius.

"If you're going to Chia-Ting," the boy piped, "what are you doing here?"

"Resting, you mangy little pig! I've come a long way." She was a virago, a shrill-voiced river girl. Her blue eyes challenged them. But the man who did all the talking still hesitated.

"Ask her—" the boy began.

The man absently gave him a flip on the head which nearly knocked him over.

"We are doing our duty. What is your name?"

"Tsin Gum."

"There is a reward for a prisoner called Wu Chi Foh. He escaped from Chia-Ting."

Tony held his breath again.

"Oh!" Yueh Hua's entire manner changed magically. "My poor father! When anyone escapes he is always punished."

"It is a big reward. You have seen no one?"

"No one. How much is the reward?"

The man hesitated, glancing at his pock-marked companion. "Fifty dollars."

Tony made a rapid mental calculation. Fifty dollars Chinese added up to about two dollars and fifty cents American. Beyond doubt, his recapture was worth more than that.

"Fifty dollars? Ooh!" Yueh Hua clapped her hands. "And my father would be so glad. What does he look like, this prisoner?"

"He is rather tall and pretends to be a fisherman. He is really a dangerous criminal. He is very ugly."

"I will look out for him all the way to Chia-Ting," Yueh Hua promised. "If I find him, will I get the reward there?"

"You haven't searched the cabin," came the boy's shrill pipe.

"Look in the cabin," the senior man directed. Then, meeting a fiery glance from Yueh Hua, "He may have slipped on board," he added weakly.

His pock-marked assistant scrambled clumsily onto the sampan, one eye on Yueh Hua. He looked in under the low, plaited roof, then climbed quickly back to the bank. "Nobody there."

They turned and walked off.

Yueh Hua rowed when Tony thought it safe to move, and nothing occurred on the way down the canal to suggest that they were being watched. When they turned into the creek, Tony saw that the left bank was a mere bamboo jungle. But the right bank showed cultivated land away to the distant hills. It was a charming view; acres of poppies, the buds just bursting into dazzling whiteness. Opium cultivation had been renewed in a big way by the Communist government.

"I'll take the oar, Yueh Hua."

"As you say, Chi Foh. But it is still dangerous."

He took the sweep, and made Yueh Hua rest. She lay down, and almost immediately fell asleep like a child.

CHAPTER SIX

From a guest house in the extensive and beautiful grounds of General Huan's summer residence, Dr. Fu-Manchu, in the gray of dawn, watched the approach of two bearers with a stretcher along a winding flower-bordered path. A third man followed. The stretcher was occupied by a motionless figure covered from head to feet with a white sheet.

The young Japanese doctor who had followed, directed the men to a room where there was a rubber-covered couch and told them to lay the patient on it. This done, the bearers, who appeared to be shivering, went away.

The Japanese removed the sheet from the motionless body. The man on the stretcher was apparently dead. He might have been Burmese, but his normal complexion had become a sort of ghastly gray. The Japanese was feeling for his pulse when Dr. Fu-Manchu came in.

"Have you selected a specimen in good condition, Matsukata?"

Matsukata bowed. "Perfect, Excellency. A former dacoit from the Shan Hills who was drafted into the Cold Corps for insubordination. He can move as silently as a cat and climb better than any cat. He is one of three who escaped recently and reached the town, creating many undesirable rumors. I selected him for his qualities and have prepared him carefully as you see."

Fu-Manchu examined the seemingly frozen body, using a stethoscope. He lifted an eyelid and peered into the fishlike eye. He nodded.

"You have prepared him well. This one will serve." He stood upright. "You may return to the clinic."

Matsukata bowed deeply and went out.

More than an hour after Yueh Hua had fallen asleep, Tony found a break in the bamboo wall bordering the creek. He had been hailed only twice from the other bank, and they were friendly hails to which he had replied cheerily. He had passed no other craft.

A narrow stream, little more than a brook, joined the creek, its surface choked with wild lilies. The bamboo jungle faded away inland. There was a sort of miniature bay. Further up he saw banyan and cypress trees.

This looked like the very place to hide the sampan until nightfall.

He swung in, tested the depth of the water and the strength of the lily stems, then pushed a way through. He found himself in a shaded pool, the water deep and crystal clear.

Yueh Hua woke up and prepared a meal which included the inevitable rice and tea. As he smoked a cigarette, Tony's eyes began to close.

"Now *you* must rest awhile," Yueh Hua insisted. "I will watch until you are ready to go on. There is an early moon tonight. It will help us to find the way."

He fell fast asleep with her words faintly ringing in his ears.

He had no idea how long he slept, nor what wakened him. But he sat up with a start and looked around.

It was night. The moon hung like a great jewel over the bamboo jungle… and he couldn't see Yueh Hua!

He got to his feet, listening, staring to right and left about the pool. He could see no one, hear nothing.

A sense of utter desolation crept over him. He was just going to call out her name. But he checked the cry in time. He crouched back under shelter of the plaited roof and stared, enthralled.

He had seen Yueh Hua.

She was swimming across the pool to a shallow bank on which they had cooked their dinner. Part of it was brightly and coldly lighted. The other part lay in shadow.

He saw her walk ashore and stand there, wringing water from her dark hair. Then she stretched her arms above her head and looked up at the sky as he had seen her do before. But that had been Yueh Hua, the river girl. This was Moon Flower, the goddess of night.

Her agility and grace he had noted. But he had never suspected that she had so slimly beautiful a body, such smooth, ivory skin and perfect limbs.

He almost ceased to breathe.

When Yueh Hua came back to the sampan after her bath, he pretended to be asleep, and let her wake him.

But the light touch of her hand affected him strangely…

On the way to Niu-fo-tu he tried to conquer the sense of awkward restraint which had come over him. He felt guilty. He rarely met Yueh Hua's glance, for he was afraid she would read his secret in his eyes.

No river girl had a body like hers.

He rowed furiously, pushing the sampan ahead as if competing in a race.

The river, when he came to it, gleamed deserted in the moonlight. The current favored him, and he made good going. He passed a tied-up junk but there seemed to be nobody on board or on watch. He couldn't see if Yueh Hua was asleep but she lay very still. A slight breeze rattled the junk's sails, making a sound like dry palm fronds in a high wind.

"Chi Foh!"

She was awake.

"Yes, Yueh Hua?"

"We have to look out for lights. Then we have to cross to the other bank and find the creek which will take us behind Niu-fo-tu. We mustn't miss it."

"Are there soldiers there, Yueh Hua?"

"No. At least, I don't think so."

"A jail?"

"No." She laughed that musical laugh. "Criminals have to be sent up to Chia-Ting."

"And that, then, is where your father takes care of them?"

He rowed on. He knew Yueh Hua was watching him, and presently she said, "Were you angry with me for being such a liar?" she asked.

"Don't be silly, Yueh Hua! I never admired you more."

"Oh."

He had said too much. Or said it the wrong way. She had spoken the "Oh" like a wondering sigh.

He decided on a policy of silence. And Yueh Hua didn't speak again. The river swept round in a long, flattened curve. Tony faintly detected a twinkling light ahead.

"Is that Niu-fo-tu, Yueh Hua?"

"No." She hesitated. "I think it must be another junk."

So she had been awake all the time!

"I hope they are all asleep."

"Let me row, Chi Foh. It is better. Don't risk being seen."

He wavered for a moment, then gave way and passed the oar over to her.

Navigation called for little but steering. The current carried them along. He crouched out of sight, watching Yueh Hua handle the long sweep with an easy grace he had never acquired. Beyond doubt, she had been born on the river.

She gave the junk as wide a berth as possible. If anybody was awake, it was someone who paid no attention. They passed unchallenged. Yueh Hua stayed at the oar, and Tony sat studying her, a silhouette against the moonlight, as she swayed rhythmically to and fro. They were silent for a long time, until she checked her rowing and stared ahead intently.

"Niu-fo-tu!" she said. "Somewhere here we turn off."

General Huan personally conducted André Skobolov to the apartment in his country residence reserved for distinguished guests.

The Russian agent, a native of a Far Eastern province, had marked Mongolian features and spoke almost flawless Chinese. He had requested his host to invite no other guests to meet him as he wished to talk business and to avoid attention. He was traveling by unfrequented roads, he explained, since he had many contacts in out-of-the-way places.

He had been entertained in a manner which recalled the magnificence of pre-Communist days, a fact upon which he congratulated General Huan so warmly that that master of cunning knew that Skobolov suspected his loyalty to the present regime.

The "business" which Skobolov discussed introduced the names of so many members of the Order of the Si-Fan that the old strategist began to wonder if Skobolov might be an expert cryptographer who had already broken the cipher in which the Si-Fan Register was written. He had carefully inspected the visitor's light baggage and had noted a large briefcase which Skobolov kept with him even during dinner. The Russian had apologized, explaining that it contained dispatches and must never be out of his sight.

General Huan bade André Skobolov good-night, regretting that some other method could not have been found to silence him, for he had a soldier's respect for brave men.

Skobolov, when the door had closed, placed the briefcase under his pillow and once more, as he had already done on his arrival, checked every item of his baggage, locked the door, examined the window which opened on a balcony overlooking the beautiful gardens, and re-examined every compartment of a large and priceless lacquered cabinet which was set against one wall.

He did this so carefully, with the aid of a flashlamp, that Dr. Fu-Manchu, who was watching his every movement through a spy-hole in a part of the cabinet which formed the back of a closet in an adjoining room, was compelled to close the aperture.

When Skobolov, who had dined and wined well, finally retired, the spacious double room became dark except for furtive moonbeams stealing through the windows.

There was a brief silence, presently broken by the snores of the sleeping man.

Fu-Manchu flashed a signal from the next room and returned to his observation post at the back of the closet.

He had watched and listened no longer than half a minute when the shadow of a man swept down past the moon-lighted window and temporarily vanished. A moment later, the shadow reappeared as the man outside stood slowly upright. He had dropped from the roof to the balcony, silent as a panther.

A nearly soundless manipulation, and the window opened. Although the night was warm, a draft of cold air penetrated the room, perceptible even at the spyhole.

The ghostly figure of the Cold Man became visible briefly in the moonlight. His body, as well as his face, had an unearthly gray tinge. He wore only a gray loincloth. His eyes were as lifeless as the eyes of a dead fish. He carried what looked like a small cage covered with gauze. Gliding nearer to the sleeping Skobolov, he removed the gauze.

A high, dim buzzing sound became audible in the suddenly chilly room.

The Cold Man, carrying the cage, crept back to the window, climbed out, and closed it. The keen ears of Dr. Fu-Manchu heard a dull thud far below. The Cold Man had dropped from the balcony to the garden where the Japanese, Matsukata, awaited him.

Dr. Fu-Manchu watched and listened.

The high-pitched droning ceased by degrees… and suddenly the sleeper awoke.

Then came a torrent of Russian curses, a sound of slapping… Skobolov was out of bed, the ray of his flashlamp shining now right, now left, now down below. With a slipper he began to kill flies, of which there seemed to be a number in the room, chasing them wherever that faint, high note led him.

When, at last, he had killed all he could find, shuddering coldly, he opened a bag and took out a tube of ointment which he began to rub onto his face, neck and arms.

Dr. Fu-Manchu closed the little trap, smiling his mirthless smile.

CHAPTER SEVEN

It was a long way up the creek to the canal behind Niu-fo-tu. And having found it, Tony had to go on for another mile or more before finding a suitable mooring where they might safely tie up. Dawn was very near by the time they made fast.

After a scant breakfast, he made Yueh Hua promise not to leave the boat until he returned. Reluctantly, she did so, and Tony set out.

He found a road lined with cypress trees which evidently led to the town. Already the sun was very hot. It promised to be a sweltering day. Soon he found himself in the shadow of one of several memorial arches which spanned the road outside the gate. Not without misgivings, for he was a marked man, he pressed on.

Entering the town, he saw the market place directly on his right, and the stalls of dealers who sold everything from sugar cane, water chestnuts, pork and pumpkins to clothing and millet whiskey.

As he turned in, expecting to get information here, a rickshaw coolie came out and nearly knocked him down.

A fat Chinese woman smoking a cigarette sat in the rickshaw. The wife of some sort of official, he judged.

"Why don't you look where you're going?" she snapped at him.

He lowered his head humbly, and passed on.

An old woman selling preserved duck stuck on long sticks and other Chinese hors d'oeuvres, gave him a toothless grin.

"There she goes. See what it is to be the wife of a jailer."

"A jailer?"

"Don't you know her? Her husband is head jailer at Chia-Ting. Give me the old days."

Head jailer at Chia-Ting. The leering brute who used to gloat over his misery. The man Yueh Hua had claimed as her father.

Yueh Hua's instincts hadn't misled her. Niu-fo-tu was dangerous.

"Can you tell me the way to the house of the Lama?" he asked.

"You can't miss it, son. Straight up the main street. The second turning on the right, and his house faces you."

He bought two of her smelly delicacies and returned to the main street.

It was just possible to see part of the waterfront, sails and masts of junks. Then, he saw the fat woman in the rickshaw. She was talking to an excited boy who stood beside her.

His heart seemed to miss a beat.

It was the cross-eyed little monster Tony thought they had shaken off.

He must make a decision—and swiftly.

The group was some distance away down the narrow, crowded street. But even so, he heard the shrill voice of the fat woman.

"Impudent liar! My daughter indeed! My husband will flog the skin off her back!"

Tony cast one swift, longing glance toward the gate, and as he did so, Mahmud, Dr. Fu-Manchu's giant bodyguard, came in.

Instinctively, Tony swung around, forced his way through a surge

64

of people hurrying in the direction of the disturbance, and plunged into a narrow and odorous alley on the right which would lead him from the point of danger. Some heads craned from windows, but they were all turned in the direction of the main street.

He cursed the hour that he had entered Niu-fo-tu for now, from behind, he heard a renewed uproar and detected the words, "Escaped prisoner! Reward."

Swift footsteps were following him. To run would be to betray himself. But he knew that his life hung in the balance. He went on walking fast. The following footsteps drew nearer. A hand touched his shoulder.

"Have you seen a man with a crutch?" came a crisp inquiry.

The password!

Gulping his relief, Tony gave the countersign. "What is the name of his crutch?"

He twisted around. The speaker was a Buddhist lama, his head closely shaved; he wore horn-rimmed glasses. The proper reply was "Freedom." But the monk gave another.

"Nayland Smith," he snapped and went on in English. "I wasn't sure, McKay, but, thank God, I was right. Your disguise is perfect. Keep calm, and keep walking. I came to look for you. Don't bother to say anything. Walk on left two blocks and the lama's house is right opposite. Jump to it. It's urgent!"

Giving Tony's arm a reassuring squeeze, Nayland Smith turned and hurried back along the way they had come.

Tony gave a parting glance to the tall figure, then turned left and hurried along the narrow street. He passed the first alley he came to, reached the second, and pulled up, staring anxiously at the house indicated.

It was an old house, the front quaintly decorated, and as he slipped into a small passage, immediately he noticed a smell of incense.

The passage was very dark. He began to walk quietly along. As his eyes became used to this gloom, he saw two doors ahead. The one directly before him was closed. The other, on the right, was open a few inches, and light showed through the cranny.

Walking on tiptoe, he reached it, hesitated…

"Please come in," a pleasant old voice invited, speaking a pure Chinese of a kind he rarely heard.

He pushed the door open.

He was in a room furnished as a library. Shelves were packed with scrolls of parchment and bound books. There was a shrine directly facing the door. Incense burned in a bronze bowl. And squatting behind a long, low table on which a yellow manuscript was spread, he saw a very old man who wore the same kind of lama robe as Nayland Smith had worn.

The old man removed his spectacles and looked up. Tony found himself being analyzed by a pair of eyes which seemed—like the dreadful eyes of Fu-Manchu—to read his thoughts. But these were kindly eyes.

There was a wooden stool near the door. He sat down and listened for sounds from the street. He had to say something.

"Your door was open, Excellency."

"My door is always open to those who may need me. Nor have I achieved excellency, my son."

Tony became tongue-tied.

"I perceive," the gentle voice went on, "that you are in some urgent danger. Give me the facts, and leave it to me to decide if I may justly help you."

"There are people out there who want to arrest me." This confession was considered quietly.

"Have you committed any crime?"

"No, my father. My only crime is that I tried to help China, where I was born."

Then, the lama smiled again and said an unexpected but welcome thing.

"Have you seen a man with a crutch?"

Tony jumped up in his glad excitement.

"What is the name of his crutch?" he asked hoarsely.

"Freedom, my son. You are welcome." He began to speak almost faultless English. "You are Captain McKay, for whom Sir Denis Nayland Smith is searching."

"By God, he found me out there and saved me from the mob!"

"He felt responsible for your safety. I hope he will join us shortly. No one saw you together?"

"I believe not. A big Nubian, who is the personal bodyguard of the man you call 'the Master' and who knows me, has just come into the town."

"Has he seen you?"

"Not to my knowledge. But there's a boy—"

He got no further. Splitting the perfumed quiet of the room, came the uproar, "Escaped prisoner! Search all the houses! Reward for whoever…"

Tony felt the sharp pang of despair. A group had gathered just outside the house. The old lama raised his hand.

"Pray don't disturb yourself, my son."

He stood up. He proved to be much taller than Tony had judged. There was quiet dignity in his bearing. He went out, leaving the door ajar. Tony reached it in one stride and stood there, breathlessly listening.

Communist China might be irreligious, but the old beliefs still swayed the masses. Sudden silence fell on the babble outside. It was broken by the gentle voice.

"What troubles you, my children?"

A chorus replied. There was a dangerous criminal hiding in the town. They were going to search all the houses.

"As you please. Search by all means—but not here. There is no criminal, dangerous or otherwise, in my house. And you are interrupting my studies."

Tony heard him coming back. He heard mutterings outside as well. But when the lama reentered the room his calm remained unruffled.

"My door is still open. But no one will come in."

"You have great courage, father, and I thank you."

The priest returned to his place behind the low table.

"Courage is a myth. There is only faith and doubt. Nor have you cause to thank me. You owe me nothing. If what I do has merit, then mine is the debt to you."

Tony dropped back on the stool, conscious of perspiration on his forehead. The noise of the crowd outside faded away. But, almost immediately, there was a swift step along the passage and Nayland Smith walked in. He nodded to Tony and addressed the old lama in English.

"Dr. Li Wu Chang, you are a magician. I was on the fringe of the crowd outside and heard you dismiss them. Those people would eat out of your hand."

"Because they know, Sir Denis, that I never told them a lie."

"Misdirection is an art." Nayland Smith grinned at Tony. "I prefer to call it magic!"

"Between you," Tony burst out, "you have saved my life. But what now?"

"First," snapped Nayland Smith, "reverting to the last report I had before you were compelled to scrap your walkie-talkie. You explored some village on the pretext of looking for a mythical relative, or somebody. You reported that you came across a large barbed-wire enclosure on the outskirts, with several buildings resembling an isolation hospital. Guards. You retired unobserved. Remember?"

"Clearly."

"What was the name of this village?"

Tony clutched his head, thought hard, and then, "Hua-Tzu," he said.

"Good," came the gentle voice of the lama. "As I suspected. That is the Soviet research plant."

Nayland Smith, a strange figure with his shaven skull and monk's robe, clapped Tony on the shoulder. "Sound work. And have you discovered the identity of the Master?"

"I have. He cross-examined me in jail. The Master is Dr. Fu-Manchu."

Half an hour later, wearing a new outfit and a bamboo hat the size of a car tire, supplied by the lama, and bending under a load of lumber, Tony set out along a narrow track formed by a dried-up ditch which ran at the foot of the lama's little garden. It joined the canal not far from the sampan.

He was sweating, his new suit soiled, when he broke out onto the bank above the boat.

"Yueh Hua. Yueh Hua."

There was no reply.

"Yueh Hua!"

He couldn't keep the sudden terror out of his voice as he jumped on board.

Then he dropped down and buried his face in his hands.

He had saved himself. But they had caught Moon Flower.

That abominable boy must have seen the boat and raced into the town to report it.

A wave of madness swept over him. He heard again the shrill voice of the fat wife of the jailer. He knew what Yueh Hua's fate would be. And he had left her to it.

There was a mist before his eyes. He clenched his teeth, tried to think. He leaped ashore like a madman and began to run. He had reached the road when he stopped running and dropped into a slow walk. Sanity, of sorts, was returning.

Why, since he still remained free, had no watch been posted over the sampan?

If only he could think clearly. He had avoided any reference to Yueh Hua during his interview with Nayland Smith and the lama. So he must handle this situation alone.

He kept on his way toward the town. His huge hat and new clothes altered his appearance, but he was sure, by now, that his enemies would be hard to deceive.

Along the road ahead, he began to count the trees; one-two-three, up to seven, then straining his eyes, looking for the little figure.

He thought miserable thoughts as he walked past a bend in the tree-lined road. Then he looked up unhappily and began counting again—one-two-three-four-five... He stood still, as if checked by a blow in the face.

A small figure was hurrying along ahead, making for the town.

As if the sound of his racing footsteps had been a dreaded warning, the figure suddenly turned aside and disappeared among banks of golden grain.

Wondering if he was going insane, if grief had led to illusion, he ran on until he came to the spot, as well as he could judge, where the disappearance had taken place. He stood panting and staring into a golden sea, billowing softly in a slight breeze.

He could find no track, see no broken stalks. Nothing stirred, except those gentle waves which passed over the sunny yellow sea.

"Yueh Hua!" he shouted hoarsely. "Yueh Hua! This is Chi Foh!"

And then the second illusion took place. Like a dark little Venus arising from golden foam, Yueh Hua stood up, not two yards from the road.

She stretched out her arms.

"Chi Foh! Chi Foh! I didn't know it was you... I thought they... I was going to look for you..."

Trampling ripe grain under his feet, Tony ran to her. Tears were streaming down her face. Her eyes shone like blue jewels.

"Moon Flower! My Moon Flower!"

He swept her close. Her heart beat against him like a hammer as he began to kiss her. He kissed her until she lay breathless in his arms.

CHAPTER EIGHT

D r. Fu-Manchu pressed a switch, and a spot of blue light disappeared from a small switchboard on the lacquered desk. He looked at General Huan, seated on a couch facing him across the room.

"Skobolov has reached Niu-fo-tu," he said softly. "So Mahmud reports. It is also suspected that the man Wu Chi Foh was seen here today. But this rumor is unconfirmed. It is possible, for we have no evidence to the contrary, that Wu Chi Foh had a rendezvous there with Skobolov; that, after all, Wu Chi Foh is a Communist agent."

Huan Tsung-Chao shook his head slightly. "This I doubt, Master, but I admit it may be so. Since Skobolov is closely covered, should they meet, Mahmud will take suitable steps."

The conversation was interrupted.

Uttering a shrill whistling sound, a tiny marmoset who had been hiding on a high ledge sprang like a miniature acrobat from there to Fu-Manchu's shoulder and began chattering angrily in his ear. The saturnine mask of that wonderful but evil face softened, melted into something almost human.

"Ah, Peko, my little friend. You are angry with me? Yet I have small sweet bananas flown all the way from Madeira for you. Is it a banana you want?"

Peko went on spitting and cursing in monkey language.

"Some nuts?"

Peko's language was dreadful.

"You are teasing him," General Huan smiled. "He is asking for his ration of my 1850 vintage rosé wine which ever since he tasted it, he has never forgotten."

Peko sprang from Fu-Manchu's shoulder onto the rug-covered floor, from there onto the shoulder of Huan. The old soldier raised his gnarled hand to caress Peko, a strange creature which he knew to be of incalculable age.

Dr. Fu-Manchu stood up, crossed to a cabinet, and took out a stoppered jar of old porcelain. With the steady hand of a pharmacist, he poured a few drops into a saucer and restopped the jar. Peko rejoined him with a whistle not of anger, but of joy, grasped the saucer, and drank deeply.

Then the uncanny little animal sprang onto the desk and began to toss manuscripts about in a joyous mood. Dr. Fu-Manchu picked him up, gently, and put him on his shoulder.

"You are a toper, Peko. And I'm not sure that is good for you. I am going to put you in your cage."

Peko escaped and leapt at one bound onto the high ledge.

"Such is the discipline," murmured Dr. Fu-Manchu, "of one of my oldest servants. It was Peko to whom I first administered my elixir, the elixir to which he and I owe our presence among men today. Did you know this, my friend?"

"I did."

Fu-Manchu studied Huan Tsung-Chao under lowered eyelids.

"Yet you have never asked me for this boon."

"I have never desired it, Master. Should you at any time observe some failure in my capacity to serve you, please tell me so. I belong to a long-lived family. My father married his sixth wife at the age of eighty."

Dr. Fu-Manchu took a pinch of snuff from a box on the desk. He began to speak, slowly, incisively.

"I have learned since my return to China that Dr. von Wehrner is the chief research scientist employed here by the Soviet. I know his work. Within his limitations, he is brilliant. But the fools who employ him will destroy the world—and all my plans—unless I can unmask and foil their schemes. Von Wehrner is the acknowledged authority on pneumonic plague. This is dangerously easy to disseminate. Its use could nearly depopulate the globe. For instance, I have a perfected preparation in my laboratory now, a mere milligram of which could end human life in Szechuan in a week."

"This is not war," General Huan said angrily. "It is mass assassination."

Fu-Manchu made a slight gesture with one long, sensitive hand. "It must never be. For several years I have had an impalpable powder which can be spread in many ways—by the winds, by individual deposits. A single shell charged with it and exploded over an area hundreds of miles in extent, would bring the whole of its human inhabitants nearly instant death."

"But you will never use it?"

"It would reduce the area to an uninhabitable desert. No living creature could exist there. What purpose would this serve? How could you, General, with all your military genius, occupy this territory?"

Huan Tsung-Chao spread his palms in a helpless gesture. "I have lived too long, Master. This is not a soldier's world. Let them close all their military academies. The future belongs to the chemists."

Dr. Fu-Manchu smiled his terrible smile.

"The experiments of those gropers who seek not to improve man's welfare, but to blot out the human race, are primitive, barbaric, childish. I have obtained complete control of one of the most powerful forces in the universe. Sound. With sound I can throw an impenetrable net over a whole city, or, if I wish, over only a part of it. No known form of aerial attack could penetrate this net. With sound I could blot out every human being in Peiping, Moscow, London, Paris or Washington, or in selected areas of those cities. For there are sounds inaudible to human ears which can destroy. I have learned to produce these lethal sounds."

Old General Huan bowed his head. "I salute the world's master mind. I know of this discovery. Its merit lies in the simple fact that such an attack would be confined to the target area and would not create a plague to spread general disaster."

"Also," Dr. Fu-Manchu added, "it would enable your troops to occupy the area immediately."

The sampan seemed like sanctuary when Tony and Yueh Hua reached it. But they knew it wasn't.

"We dare not stay here until sunset, Chi Foh. They are almost sure to search the canal."

She lay beside him, her head nestled against his shoulder. He stroked her hair. Tony knew he had betrayed himself when he had called out in his mad happiness, "Moon Flower"—in English. But, if Yueh Hua had noticed, she had given no sign. Perhaps, in her excitement, she had not heard the revealing words.

"I know," he said. "I expect they are looking for us now. But what can we do?"

"If we could reach Lung Chang we should be safe," she spoke

dreamily. "It is not far to Lung Chang."

He nodded. Oddly enough, Nayland Smith's instructions had been for him to abandon his boat and hurry overland to Lung Chang. He was to report there to a certain Lao Tse-Mung, a contact of Sir Denis's and a man of influence.

"What I think we should do, Chi Foh, is to go on up this canal and away from the river. They are not likely to search in that direction. If we can find a place to hide until nightfall, then we could start for Lung Chang, which is only a few miles inland."

Tony considered this plan. He laughed and kissed Yueh Hua. This new happiness, with fear of a dreadful death hanging over them, astonished him.

"What should I do without you, Yueh Hua?"

They started without delay. It was very hot, and Tony welcomed his large sun hat, gift of the lama. He worked hard, and Yueh Hua insisted upon taking her turn at the oar. There was no sign of pursuit.

In the late afternoon Yueh Hua found a perfect spot to tie up; a little willow-shadowed creek. There was evidence, though, that they were near a village, for through the trees they could see a road along which workers were trudging homeward from the fields.

"It will do," Tony agreed, "for we shall never be noticed here. But soon I'm going to explore a little way to try to find out just where we are!"

When they had moored the sampan they shared a meal, and Tony went ashore to take a look around.

He discovered that they were moored not more than a few hundred yards from the village, which only a screen of bamboos concealed from them. It was an insignificant little group of dwellings, but it boasted an inn of sorts which spanned the road along which they had seen the peasants walking homeward. He returned and reported this to Yueh Hua.

"I think we should start for Lung Chang at once," she advised. "The fields are deserted now, and soon dusk will come. I believe I can find the way if we go back a mile or so nearer to Niu-fo-tu."

Tony loved her more and more every hour they were together. Her keen intelligence made her a wonderful companion. Her beauty, which he had been slow to recognize, had completely conquered him.

"Let's wait a little while longer, Yueh Hua," he said yearningly. "I want to tell you how much I love you." He took her in his arms. "Kiss me while I try."

His try was so successful that dusk was very near when Yueh Hua sighed, "My dear one, it is time we left here."

Tony reluctantly agreed. They pushed the boat out again to the canal and swung around to head back toward Niu-fo-tu.

Tony had dipped the blade of the oar and was about to begin work when he hesitated, lifted the long sweep, and listened.

Someone was running down to the canal, forcing a way through undergrowth, and at the same time uttering what sounded like breathless sobs. It was a man, clearly enough, and a man in a state of blind panic.

"Chi Foh." Yueh Hua spoke urgently. "Be quick. We must get away. Do you hear it?"

"Yes. I hear it. But I don't understand."

A gasping cry came. The man evidently had sighted the boat. "Save me! Help, boatman!"

Then Tony heard him fall, heard his groans. He swung the boat into the bank. "Take the oar, Yueh Hua, while I see what's wrong here."

Yueh Hua grasped him. "Chi Foh! You are mad. It may be a

trap. We know we are being followed."

Gently, he broke away. "My dearest—give me my gun—you know where it is."

From the locker Yueh Hua brought the .38. She was trembling excitedly. Tony knew that it was for his safety, not for her own, that she was frightened. He kissed her, took the pistol, and jumped ashore.

Groans and muffled hysterical words led him to the spot. He found a half-dressed figure writhing in a tangle of weeds two to three feet high; a short, thickset man of Slavonic type, and although not lacking in Mongolian characteristics, definitely not Chinese. He was clutching a bulging briefcase. He looked up.

"A hundred dollars to take me to Huang-ko-shu!" he groaned. "Be quick."

Tony dragged the man to his feet. He discovered that his hands were feverishly hot. "Come on board. I can take you part of the way."

He half carried the sufferer, still clutching his leather case, onto the sampan.

"Chi Foh, you are insane," was Yueh Hua's greeting. "What are we to do with him?"

"Put him ashore somewhere near a town. He's very ill." He dragged the unwanted passenger under the mat roof and took to the oar.

But again he hesitated, although only for a moment. There were cries, running footsteps, swiftly approaching from the direction of the hidden village.

CHAPTER NINE

Tony drove the sampan at racing speed. He could only hope that they were out of sight before the party, evidently in pursuit of their passenger, had reached the canal.

The banks were deserted. Moonlight transformed poppy fields into seas of silver. When, drawing near to Niu-fo-tu, grain succeeded poppy, the prospect became even more fairylike. It was a phantom journey, never to be forgotten, through phantom landscapes. Willows bordering the canal were white ghosts on one bank, black ghosts on the other.

Yueh Hua crouched beside him. The man they had rescued had apparently gone mad. He struck out right and left in his delirium, slapping his face and hands as if tormented by a swarm of mosquitoes.

"Chi Foh," Yueh Hua whispered, "he is very ill. Could it be—" she hesitated—"that he has the *plague*?"

"No, no, don't think such things. He shows no signs of having the plague. Take the oar for a few minutes, my dearest. He must want water."

"Oh, Chi Foh."

Tony clasped her reassuringly and ducked in under the low roof. He was far from confident, himself, about what ailed the mysterious passenger, but human feeling demanded that he do his best for him.

The man sipped water eagerly; he was forever trying to drive away imaginary flying things which persecuted him. His head rested on his bulky briefcase. His hectic mutterings were in a language which Tony didn't know. To questions in Chinese he made no reply. Once only he muttered, "Huang-ko-shu."

Tony returned to Yueh Hua. "Tell me, where is Huang-ko-shu?"

"It is on the Yangtze River many miles below Lung Chang."

"I told him I would take him part of the way," Tony murmured. "We must put him ashore when we get across, Yueh Hua."

"I wish we had never found him," she whispered, giving up the oar to Tony.

They passed their old mooring place behind Niu-fo-tu and at last reached the river. Tony had insisted on doing most of the rowing and was coming close to exhaustion.

The Lu Ho looked deserted.

"Let me take the oar," Yueh Hua said gently, but insistently. "There is very little current and I can cross quite easily. You must, Chi Foh."

He gave in. He watched Yueh Hua at the long sweep, swinging easily to its movement with the lithe grace of a ballerina. What a woman!

Tony found it hard to keep awake. The man they had rescued had stopped raving, become quite silent. The gentle movement of the boat, the rhythmic swish of the long oar, did their hypnotic work. He fell asleep…

"Chi Foh." Yueh Hua's voice. "Wake up. I am afraid."

Tony was wide awake before she stopped speaking. He drew her down to him. "Where are we? What's happened?"

He looked around in the darkness. The boat was tied up in a silent backwater. Through the motionless leaves of an overhanging tree which looked like a tree carved in ebony, he could see the stars.

"We are on the left bank, Chi Foh. Lung Chang is not many miles away. But—the man is dead!"

Tony got to his feet. He had a flashlight in the locker; he groped his way to it, found it, and shone its light on the man who lay there.

Beyond doubt, Yueh Hua was right. Their passenger was dead. Yueh Hua knew that Tony had an automatic pistol, but he had hidden the flashlight. He wondered if she would say something about it, and tried to think of an explication. But she said nothing.

Tony searched the man's scanty clothing, but found no clue to his identity. In a body belt, which he unfastened, there was a considerable sum of money, but nothing else. The big portfolio was locked, and there was no key. This far he had gone when Yueh Hua called out, "Throw him overboard, Chi Foh. He may have died of plague."

But Tony, who had a smattering of medical knowledge, knew that he had not died of the plague.

"Don't worry, Yueh Hua. I told you before, there's no question of plague. I must try to find out who he was."

He went to work on the lock of the briefcase and ultimately succeeded in breaking it. He found it stuffed with correspondence in Russian, a language of which he knew nothing, much of it from the Kremlin and some from the Peiping Embassy, this fact clearly indicated by the embossed headings on the stationery. The man was a Soviet agent.

There was also a bound book containing a number of manuscript papers in Chinese, which, although he knew written Chinese, Tony was unable to decipher.

He put the book and the correspondence back in the broken

briefcase and dropped the briefcase in the locker.

The body of the dead Russian had to be disposed of. This was clear enough. When it was found, and eventually it would be found, the evidence must suggest that he had fallen into the hands of thieves who had taken whatever he had had in his possession. Therefore, the money belt must not be found on him.

Tony removed the belt, then switched off the flashlight and rejoined Yueh Hua who was watching him, wide-eyed.

"Can we reach Lung Chang by water from here, Yueh Hua?"

"No, Chi Foh. We can go up this canal a little way further. Then, we must take to the road. But—"

"Is it a straight road?"

"There are no straight roads in China."

He forced a laugh and kissed her. "All the same, that's what we must do. Somewhere, I am going to throw the dead man overboard."

"That is right," Yueh Hua agreed. "We need not carry much. When we get to Lung Chang, my aunt will take care of us. But"—she drew back—"you will lose your boat."

Tony was baffled. "I must take a chance. I have some money left... or I might steal another sampan, as you meant to steal mine."

He pushed the boat out of the little backwater and headed upstream. Yueh Hua, he knew, was unusually high-strung. She watched him in a queer way he didn't like. At a point on the deserted canal where there was a sort of waterway crossroads, he stopped rowing.

"Take the oar, Yueh Hua. I'm going to dump him overboard."

Some hazy idea that prayers should be said at such a time flashed through his mind. He dismissed the idea. It was impractical, in the first place. Secondly, the dead man, as a Soviet Communist, was an atheist. He dragged the half-clad body out and dropped it in the canal.

"May God have mercy on your soul," he whispered.

They rowed on to a spot where a footbridge spanned the canal. Yueh Hua studied the situation carefully.

"There is a path from this bridge, Chi Foh, which leads to a main road—the road to Lung Chang."

Tony forced a laugh. "So this is where we say goodbye to our boat. It's too shallow to sink it here. We shall have to take a chance and just leave it."

"Oh, Chi Foh, my darling." She threw her arms around him. "We have been so happy on this little boat."

Tony loved her for the words, but immediately became practical again.

"We'll drop whatever we don't want overboard and pack up the rest. I can carry the big bundles on this bamboo rod and you can carry what's left in the old basket..."

Yueh Hua going ahead as arranged and Tony following, still adorned with his huge bamboo hat, they started on the last leg of their journey to Lung Chang.

The road, when they came to it, didn't look particularly dangerous, except to motorists. One thing was certain. At that hour, it carried little traffic.

He had plenty of opportunity for thinking. Yueh Hua, he knew, had become an indispensable part of his life. He didn't mean to lose her, whatever she was, wherever she came from.

Even if this amounted to changing his career, he would marry her. He could live with Yueh Hua on a desert island and be happy. She could be happy, too. She had proved it.

He heard an automobile coming swiftly from behind.

Stepping to the side of the neglected road, he let it go by. He moved just in time. It passed at racing speed, a new Buick. He never got a glimpse of the driver. Such speed, on such a road, betrayed urgency.

Yueh Hua was waiting for him by a bend ahead. He saw that she was frightened.

"In that car. The man with green eyes. The big black was driving."

This was staggering news.

It might mean, as he had feared, that Dr. Fu-Manchu had learned of his contact in Lung Chang!

He longed to take Yueh Hua into his confidence. Her knowledge of the place, her acute intelligence, her intuition, would be invaluable now. But he was bound to silence.

The road here passed through an area of unreclaimed land where nature had taken over. They were in a jungle. They found their way to a spot where the fallen branch of a tree offered a seat. Dropping their loads, they sat down. He looked at Yueh Hua. There was no gladness in her eyes.

"Chi Foh, they know where we are going. *He* will be waiting for us in Lung Chang."

But, as Tony watched her, the mystery of Yueh Hua was uppermost in his mind. It was hard to believe that Fu-Manchu could have conceived such a burning passion for the grubby little girl Yueh Hua had then appeared to be, that he would be driven to this frantic chase.

He dismissed the supposition. He himself was the quarry. Perhaps he had made some mistake. Perhaps those hypnotic eyes had read more than he suspected. Dr. Fu-Manchu had planned to interview him again. Nayland Smith had saved him. But the fact that news of the reward for his capture had been flashed to so many centers indicated that Fu-Manchu knew more than he had credited him with knowing.

Tony put his arm around the dejected little figure beside him. "Tell me more about your friends in Lung Chang, Yueh Hua. If we can get to them, shall we be safe?"

"As safe as we can hope to be, Chi Foh. My aunt is an old, retired servant of the Lao family."

"Does your aunt live right in the town?"

"No. In a small house on the estate. It is a mile from Lung Chang."

"This side, or beyond?"

"This side, Chi Foh."

"We have a chance, even if they have found the boat. They won't be watching your aunt's house. And we have to get there—fast."

CHAPTER TEN

It became a forced march. Twice they took cover; once, while a heavily loaded bullock cart went lumbering by, and again when they were nearly overtaken by an old jeep in which four soldiers were traveling toward Lung Chang.

Dawn was not far off when they reached a point in a long, high wall which had bordered the road for over half a mile. Dimly, he saw Yueh Hua stand still and beckon to him. He hurried forward.

She stood before a heavy, ornamental gate through which he could see a large, rambling building partly masked in ornamental gardens—a typical Chinese mansion—on a slope beyond. The high wall evidently surrounded the property.

"My uncle was Lao Tse-Mung's gardener," Yueh Hua explained. "He and his wife always lived here, and my aunt is allowed to stay."

"Is that Lao Tse-Mung's house over there?"

"Yes, Chi Foh. Please wait outside for a little while where they can't see you, until I explain"—she hesitated for a second—"who you are."

Yueh Hua had led him to the very door of the man he had to see! He saw her reach inside the gate. An interval, footsteps, then a woman's cry—a cry of almost hysterical gladness.

"My baby! My Yueh Hua!"

The gate was unlocked. The voice died away into unintelligible babbling as they went in.

This gave him something else to think about.

Evidently Yueh Hua had told him her real name. But why had Yueh Hua asked him to wait, and gone in first herself?

In any case, he didn't have to wait long. She came running back for him.

"I haven't told her, Chi Foh, about us. But she knows how wonderful you have been to me."

This clearly was true. Tears were streaming down her aunt's face when Yueh Hua brought him into the little house, evidently a gate-lodge. She seemed to want to kneel at his feet. He wondered what the exact relationship could be between Yueh Hua and Mai Cha, her aunt. It would have been hard to find two people less similar in type than this broad-faced old peasant woman and Yueh Hua. But Mai Cha became Tony's friend on sight, for it was plain that she adored Yueh Hua.

She left them together while she went to prepare a meal. But Yueh Hua, who seemed to have become suddenly and unaccountably shy, went out to help her.

He walked quietly under the flowered porch and looked across to the big house and its setting of arches, bridges, and formal gardens. He could be there in five minutes. A winding path, easy to follow in starlight, led up to the house.

Yueh Hua had reached sanctuary, but Tony's business was with Lao Tse-Mung. He couldn't hope to avoid exposure of his real identity to Yueh Hua once he had reported to the friend of Nayland Smith. This he must face.

But, the major problem remained. Where was Dr. Fu-Manchu?

Had this man, who seemed to wield supreme power in the province, out-maneuvered Sir Denis? He could not expect the late gardener's widow to know anything of what had happened tonight in the big house.

He must watch his step.

There were several little bridges to cross and many steps to climb before he reached a terrace which ran the whole length of the house. Flowering vines draped a pergola. Some night-scented variety gave out a strong perfume. He wondered where the main entrance was located, and if he should try to find it.

He stood still for a moment, listening.

A murmur of conversation reached him. There were people in some nearby room. Step by step, he crept closer, hugging shadowy patches where the vines grew thickly. Three paces more and he would be able to look in.

But he didn't take the three paces. He stopped dead.

An icy chill seemed to run down his spine.

He had heard a voice, pitched in a clear, imperious tone.

"We have no time to waste."

It was the voice of *Dr. Fu-Manchu!*

He had walked into a trap.

Tony checked a mad panorama of thoughts racing across his brain. Nayland Smith would gain something after all. He fingered the automatic which he had kept handy in a waist belt and moved stealthily forward. Whatever his own end might be, he could at least remove the world menace of Dr. Fu-Manchu.

He could see into the room now.

It was furnished, in true Chinese fashion, but with great luxury.

Almost directly facing him, on a divan backed by embroidered draperies, he saw a white-bearded figure wearing a black robe and a beaded black cap. A snuff bowl lay before him.

Facing the old mandarin so that his back was toward the terrace, someone sat in a dragon-legged armchair. His close-cropped hair showed the massive skull beneath.

Dr. Fu-Manchu.

The mandarin's eyes were half-closed, but suddenly he opened them. He looked fixedly toward the terrace, and straight at Tony.

Holding a pinch of snuff between finger and thumb and still looking directly at him, he waved his hand gracefully in a sweeping side gesture as he raised the snuff to his nostrils.

But Tony had translated the gesture.

It meant that he had moved too close. He could be seen from the room.

Quickly he stepped to the right. A wave of confidence surged through him.

This was Lao Tse-Mung who sat watching him, who had known him instantly for what he was, who had warned him of his danger. A highly acute and unusual character.

Tony could still see him clearly through a screen of leaves.

The mandarin spoke in light, easy tones.

"This is the first time you have honored my poor roof, Excellency, in many moons. To what do I owe so great a privilege?"

"I am rarely in Lung Chang," was the sibilant reply. "I see that it might have been wise to come more often."

"My poor hospitality is always at my friends' disposal."

"Doubtless." Fu-Manchu's voice sank to a venomous whisper. "Your hospitality to members of the present regime is less certain."

Lao Tse-Mung smiled slightly, settling himself among his

cushions. "I retired long ago from the world of politics, Excellency. I give all my time to the cultivation of my vines."

"Some of them grow thorns, I believe?"

"Many of them."

"Myself, Lao Tse-Mung, I also cultivate vines. I seek to restore to the garden of China its old glory. And so I fertilize the human vines which are fruitful and tear out those which are parasites, destructive. Let us come to the point."

Lao Tse-Mung's far-seeing eyes sought among the shadows for Tony.

Tony understood. He was to listen closely.

"My undivided attention is at your disposal, Excellency."

"A man calling himself Wu Chi Foh, who is a dangerous spy, escaped from the jail at Chia-Ting and was later reported to be near Lung Chang. He may be carrying vital information dangerous to the Peiping regime." Fu-Manchu's voice became the familiar hiss. "I wonder if you, perhaps, have news of Wu Chi Foh."

Lao Tse-Mung's expression remained bland, unmoved.

"I can only assure Excellency that I have no news concerning this Wu Chi Foh. Are you suggesting that I am acquainted with this man?"

Dr. Fu-Manchu's voice rose on a note of anger. "Your record calls for investigation. As a former high official, you have been allowed privileges. I merely suggest that you have abused them."

"My attention remains undivided, Excellency. I beg you to make your meaning clearer."

Tony knew that his fate, and perhaps the fate of Lao Tse-Mung, hung in the balance. He knew, too, that he could never have fenced with such an adversary as Fu-Manchu, under the X-ray scrutiny of those green eyes, with the imperturbable serenity of the old mandarin.

"Subversive elements frequent your house."

"The news distresses me." Lao Tse-Mung took up a hammer which hung beside a small gong. "Permit me to assemble my household for your inspection."

"Wait." The word was spoken imperatively. "There are matters I have to discuss with you, personally. For example, you maintain a private airfield on your estate."

Lao Tse-Mung smiled. His smile was directed toward Tony, whom his keen eyes had detected through the cover of leaves.

"I am sufficiently old fashioned to prefer the ways of life of my ancestors, but sufficiently up-to-date to appreciate the convenience of modern transport." Lao Tse-Mung calmly took another pinch of snuff, smiling his sly smile. "I may add that in addition to chairs and rickshaws, I have also several automobiles. We are a long way from the railhead, Excellency, and some of my guests come from distant provinces."

"I wish to inspect this airfield. Also, the garage."

"It will be an honor and a great joy to conduct you. Let us first visit the airstrip, which is some little distance from the house. Then, as you wish, we can visit the garage. Your own car is there at present. And, as the garage is near the entrance gate, and I know Excellency's time is valuable"—the shrewd old eyes were staring straight into Tony's through the darkness—*"there should be no unnecessary delay."*

This statement was astonishing to Tony because it was unmistakably a direct order to *him.*

He accepted it.

Silently, he slipped away from the lighted window, back along the terrace, and began to run headlong down the slope to the gate lodge.

Old Mai Cha was standing in her doorway.

"Quick, get Yueh Hua. There's not a minute to spare."

"She has already gone, Chi Foh."

"Gone!" He stood before her, stricken, unable to understand.

"Yes, Chi Foh. But she is safe. You will see her again very soon. She has taken all you brought with you in your bundles. You know they are in good keeping."

He grasped Mai Cha by the shoulders, drawing her close, peering into her face. Her love for Moon Flower he couldn't doubt. But what was she hiding?

"Is this true, Mai Cha?"

"I swear it, in the name of my father, Chi Foh. I can tell you no more, except that my orders are to lead you to the garage. A car is waiting. You must hurry—for Yueh Hua's sake and for your own. Please follow me."

Even in that moment of danger, of doubt, he was struck by the fact that she showed no surprise, only a deep concern. She seemed to be expecting this to happen. She was no longer an emotional old woman. She was controlled, practical.

A long, gently sloping path led them to a tiled yard upon which a lighted garage opened. One car, a sleek Rolls, with lights off, stood in the yard. He saw two other cars in the garage beyond.

Mai Cha opened the door of the Rolls, and Tony tumbled in. She kissed his hand as he closed the door. In the light from the garage behind he saw the back of a driver, a broad-shouldered Chinese with a shaven skull. The car started. Smoothly, they moved out of the paved yard.

"Thank God you're safe, McKay," came a snappy voice.

The driver was Nayland Smith.

CHAPTER ELEVEN

"Don't worry about Lao Tse-Mung, McKay. He has the guile of the serpent and the heart of a great patriot. He could convince men like us that night is day, that a duck is a swan. He called me an hour ago, and all's well. This isn't his first brush with the Master, and my money was on Tse-Mung all along. By the way, what about another drink?"

Tony grinned feebly, watching Nayland Smith mix drinks. It was hard to relax, even now, to accept the fact that, temporarily, he was safe. He glanced down at a clean linen suit which had taken the place of his Chinese costume and wondered afresh at the efficient underground network of which he had become a member.

This charming bungalow on a hill overlooking Chungking was the property of the great English drug house of Roberts & Benson and was reserved for the use of their chief buyer, Ray Jenkins, who operated from the firm's office in the town. Nayland Smith handed him a glass.

"You'll like Jenkins," Sir Denis rapped in his staccato fashion. "Sound man. And what he doesn't know about opium, even Dr. Fu-

Manchu couldn't teach him. He buys only the best, and Chungking is the place to get it."

He dropped into a split-cane chair and began to fill his pipe. He wore a well-cut linen suit and would have looked his familiar self but for the shaven skull. Noting Tony's expression, he laughed boyishly.

Tony laughed, too, and was glad that he could manage it; for in spite of Mai Cha's assurance, he was desperately worried about Moon Flower. And inquiries were out of the question.

"I can only thank you again, Sir Denis, for all you have done."

"Forget it, McKay. The old lama is one of ours, and he had orders to look out for you. Your last message had warned me that you expected to be arrested and I notified him. Then, I put Lao Tse-Mung in charge until I arrived."

"This is amazing, Sir Denis. I begin to hope that China will shake off the Communists yet."

Nayland Smith nodded grimly; lighted his pipe. "From my point of view, there are certain advantages in our recognition of the Peiping crowd. For instance, I can travel openly in China, but I avoid Szechuan."

"How right you are."

"Lao Tse-Mung, of course, is our key man in the province. The job calls for enormous courage, and something like genius. He has both. He master-minded the whole affair of getting you out of jail. The lama, who has more degrees than you could count on your fingers, gave you your instructions. He speaks and writes perfect English. Also, he has contacts inside the jail. We're not washed up yet in the East, McKay."

"So it seems."

Nayland Smith tugged at the lobe of his ear, a habit Tony knew indicated deep reflection. "If Fu-Manchu can enlist the anti-

Communist elements," he said, "the control of this vast country may pass into his hands. This would pose another problem. But let's cross that bridge when we come to it. This bungalow is one of our bases. It was here that I converted myself into a lama. Jenkins provided me with a vintage Ford, a useful bus on Chinese roads. You see, there's constant coming and going of Buddhist priests across the Burma frontier, and if my Chinese is shaky, my Burmese is sound." He glanced at his watch. "Jenkins is late. Feeling hungry?"

"No." Tony shook his head. "After my first bath for weeks in a civilized bathroom, a change of clothes and a drink, I feel delightfully relaxed."

"Good for you. Jenkins has another guest who is probably reveling in a warm bath, too, after a long journey; Jeanie Cameron-Gordon. Her father, an old friend of mine, is the world-famous medical entomologist, Dr. Cameron-Gordon. His big work on sleeping sickness and the tsetse fly is the textbook for all students of tropical medicine. Ran a medical mission. But more later."

"Whatever brings his daughter here?" Tony wanted to know.

Before Nayland Smith could reply, the stout, smiling, and capable resident Chinese housekeeper, whom Tony had met already, came in. She was known simply as Mrs. Wing. She bowed.

"Miss Cameron-Gordon," she said, in her quaint English, "is dressed, and asks if she should join you, or if you are in a business conference."

Nayland Smith smiled broadly. "The conference is over, Mrs. Wing. Please ask Miss Jeanie to join us."

Mrs. Wing bowed again, went out, and a moment later Miss Cameron-Gordon came in, her face shaded by a wide-brimmed hat. She wore a tailored suit of cream shantung which perfectly fit her beautiful figure.

For an interval that couldn't be measured in terms of time, Tony stood rigid. Then he sprang forward.

Miss Jeanie Cameron-Gordon found herself locked in his arms.

"Moon Flower! Moon Flower!"

"I had an idea," Nayland Smith said dryly, "that you two might be acquainted."

Ray Jenkins joined them for lunch. A thin Chinese-yellow man with large, wiry hands, gaunt features, and a marked Cockney accent, he had a humorous eye and a markedly self-confident manner. Moon Flower was reserved and embarrassed, avoiding Tony's looks of admiration. He felt he was the cause of this and cursed the impulse which had prompted him to betray their intimacy. He didn't attempt to deny that he was in love with her, but gave a carefully edited account of their meeting and how he had formed a deep affection for his native helper.

"I never saw Jeanie in her other kit," Jenkins said nasally. He called one and all by their first names. "But, looking at her now, Tony, I should say you were nuts not to know she wasn't Chinese."

"But I am," Moon Flower told him, "on my mother's side."

Ray Jenkins regarded her for a long time, then, "God's truth," he remarked. "Your mother must have been a stunner."

Nayland Smith threw some light upon what had happened at Lao Tse-Mung's. He had arrived there several hours before Tony, intending to proceed with speed to Chungking as soon as Tony showed up. He found the mandarin in an unhappy frame of mind. The daughter of his old friend, Dr. Cameron-Gordon, who had been staying at his house, had disappeared. He suspected that she had gone in search of information about her father, contrary to his, Lao Tse-Mung's advice. He had used all the facilities at his disposal, but with no result.

"I'll leave it to Moon Flower, as you call Jeanie, to tell you the whole story, McKay," Sir Denis said, with one of his impish grins. "She will tell it better than I can."

Moon Flower gave him a reproachful, but half-playful glance.

"I was staggered," he went on. "I had heard in Hong Kong that her father died in a fire which destroyed the medical mission building. But I supposed that Jeanie was still in England. I was discussing the problem of Jeanie's disappearance with Tse-Mung when his secretary ran in and announced, 'The Master is here!'

"Fast action was called for. I made my way back toward the entrance gate. From behind a bank of rhododendrons I had the pleasure of seeing my old friend Dr. Fu-Manchu, wearing what looked like a Prussian uniform, striding up to the house. A big Nubian, whom I had seen somewhere before, followed him."

"You probably saw him in Niu-fo-tu," Tony broke in. "I was running away from him when you spoke to me."

"Possibly. Fu-Manchu's car, a Buick, still hot, was in the garage. It was parked alongside a majestic Rolls belonging to Lao Tse-Mung. My old Ford stood ready in the yard. What to do next was a problem. I had to stand by until you arrived. But I had to keep out of the way of Fu-Manchu, as well. I thought up several plans to intercept you, when suddenly they were all washed out."

"What happened?" Tony asked excitedly.

"My walkie-talkie came to life. Tse-Mung's secretary reported that Jeanie and a Chinese companion, Chi Foh, were in the gate-lodge! I had arranged with Tse-Mung, if I should miss you and you appeared at the house, to direct you to the garage. But I hadn't expected Jeanie.

"I quickly told Sun Shao-Tung, the secretary, to send me a driver who knew the way to Chungking, to order the man to stand by the Ford in the garage. Then I headed for the gate-lodge. Mai Cha told me that Moon Flower was in the bedroom sorting out some clothes and I had Moon Flower away with her bundle of dresses in five minutes. Am I right, Jeanie?"

"Yes," Moon Flower agreed, and her eyes told her gratitude. "You certainly drove me remorselessly."

"And so here you are. God knows where you'd be if Dr. Fu-Manchu had found you. The driver was standing by, as ordered, and off you went in my Ford to Ray Jenkins, a harbor in any storm."

"Thanks a lot," Ray Jenkins said. "Drinks all round, if I may say so."

"Your absence, McKay," Sir Denis added, "was an unexpected headache. But you have told me how Tse-Mung handled a difficult situation. And so, for the moment, Dr. Fu-Manchu is baffled."

On the flower-covered porch of the bungalow, with a prospect of snowy poppy fields below extending to the distant foothills, Tony at last found himself alone with Moon Flower. She lay beside him, in a long cane chair, smoking a cigarette and no longer evading his looks of adoration.

"We're a pair of terrible liars, aren't we?" she said softly, and the sound of her musical voice speaking English made his heart glad.

"I'm still in a daze, Moon Flower. I seem to have come out of a wonderful dream. And I still don't know where the dream ends and real life begins. I know, of course, that you're not a Chinese girl and you know I'm not a fisherman from Hong Kong. I never suspected that you weren't what you pretended to be, but I often thought you had doubts about me."

"How right you were, Chi Foh. And to me you'll always be Chi Foh. But it was a long time before doubts came. That part is all over now, and I think I'm sorry."

Tony reached across urgently and grasped her arm. "You don't regret an hour of it, Moon Flower?"

"Not one minute," she whispered.

"You know I learned to adore you as Yueh Hua, don't you? I had planned to risk everything and to marry my little river girl. After all I was just doing a job I had volunteered to do. But your motive was a sad one—your father."

"Let me tell you about it in my own way, Chi Foh. It is sad, yes; but now, there is hope." Jeanie stubbed out her cigarette. "You see, Lao Tse-Mung is my grand uncle. My father, Dr. Cameron-Gordon, married Lao Tse-Mung's niece. So, you see, I am really partly Chinese."

"No more than I am," Tony broke in. "My mother's mother was Chinese, too. That's why I can pass as Chinese, myself."

Jeanie continued, "My father, of course, had traveled all over the world and become well known for his work. Then, he came to China to study diseases here. He met my mother. She was a very beautiful woman, Chi Foh. He married her. For her sake, I believe, he accepted the post as director of the medical mission at Chien Wei. The mission used to stand by the Pool of Lily Dreams. Do you remember the Pool of Lily Dreams?"

"Can I ever forget it?"

"I was born there, Chi Foh. Mai Cha was my nurse, and I was allowed to play with her son, who is now living in the United States and has become very prosperous. He taught me to handle a sampan, and of course I picked up the local dialect. My mother taught me pure Chinese. When I grew up, I was sent to school in England."

She stopped. Tony found her hand, and held it. "What then, Moon Flower?"

"My mother died. The news nearly killed me, for I worshipped her. I came back. Oh, Chi Foh, I found everything so changed. My poor father was still distracted by the loss of my mother, and the Communist authorities had begun to persecute him because he openly defied their orders."

Moon Flower opened her cigarette case, but changed her mind and closed it again. "He wouldn't let me stay at the mission. He insisted that I return to my aunt in Hong Kong and wait there until he joined me. He knew the Communists meant to close the mission, but he wasn't ready to go."

"So you went back to Hong Kong?"

"Yes. We had two letters. Then—silence. We tried to find out what had happened. Our letters to Lao Tse-Mung were never answered. At last, and the shock nearly drove me mad, came news that the mission had been burned down, that my father was believed to have died in the fire. My aunt couldn't stop me. I started at once."

Tony wanted to say, "How glad I am you did," but was afraid to break Moon Flower's train of thought, and so said nothing.

"I went to Lung Chang, to my uncle's house. I asked him why he had not answered my letters, and he told me he had never received them. He tried to make me understand that China was now a police state, that no one's correspondence was safe. He confirmed the news that the mission had been burned, but he suspected my father was still alive—probably under arrest."

Moon Flower, now, was fired with enthusiasm and indignation. She opened her cigarette case again, and this time took one out and allowed Tony to light it.

"My Uncle Tse-Mung advised caution, and patience. But I wasn't in the mood for either. Wearing a suit of peasant clothes belonging to Mai Cha, but taking some money of my own, I slipped out early one morning and made my way, as a Chinese working girl, to what had been my home. Oh, Chi Foh—"

Moon Flower dropped her cigarette in a tray and lay back with closed eyes.

"I think I understand," he said softly.

"Nothing was left, but ashes and broken lumber. All our furniture, everything we possessed, all the medical stores, had been burned, stolen, or destroyed. I was walking away from the nuns when I had the good luck to see an old woman I remembered, one of my father's patients. I knew she was a friend, but I thought she was going to faint when she recognized me. She gave me news which saved me from complete collapse."

"What was it, Moon Flower?"

"My father had not died. He had been arrested as a spy and taken away. She advised me to try to get information at a summer villa not far from Chia-Ting, owned by Huan Tsung-Chao, Communist governor of the province. Her daughter, Shun-Hi, who had been a nurse in the mission hospital, was employed at the villa. I remembered Shun-Hi. And so, of course, I made my way up to Chia-Ting. But my money was running short. When at last I found the villa, a beautiful place surrounded by acres of gardens, I didn't quite know what to do."

Tony was learning more and more about the intrepid spirit of his little companion on the sampan with every word she spoke. She was indeed a treasure, and he found it hard to believe that such a pearl had been placed in his keeping.

"There were many servants," Moon Flower went on, "and some of them didn't live in the villa. I watched near the gate by which these girls came out in the evening. And at last I saw Shun-Hi. She walked toward the town, and I followed her until I thought we were alone. Then I spoke to her. She recognized me at once, began to cry, and nearly went down on her knees."

Moon Flower took her smoldering cigarette from the ashtray and went on smoking.

"But I found out what I wanted to know. My father *was* alive. He was under house arrest and working in a laboratory attached to the villa. The Master was a guest of Huan Tsung-Chao! I had very little money left and nothing but my gratitude to offer Shun-Hi, but I begged her to try to let my father know that I was waiting for a message from him."

"Did she do it?"

"Yes, thank God. I shared her room that night and wrote a letter to my father. And the next evening she smuggled a note from him out to me. It said that I should go to Lao Tse-Mung who would get me to Hong Kong where I could then apply to British authorities and tell them the facts. My father wrote that he was in the hands of Dr. Fu-Manchu, adding, 'Now known as *the Master*.' He told me that at all costs I must get away from, in his own words, 'that devil incarnate.' He warned me not to let anyone even suspect my identity."

"Moon Flower, my dearest, what did you do next?"

"I went down to the river to see if I could find someone to take me part of the way. But I had no luck at all… and the police began to watch *me*. Finally, I was arrested as a suspicious character and thrown into jail."

"That hideous jail!"

"Yes, Chi Foh. They wouldn't believe the story I told them. It was the same story that I told *you*. They punished me."

"The swine!" Tony burst out. "It was Soong?"

"Yes. I screamed."

"I heard you."

The blue eyes were turned to him. "How could you hear me? Where were you?"

"I was a prisoner, too. And I heard your scream in that ghastly place."

"So did the prison governor, a friend of my father's. He came to see me. He released me. He could do no more. It was just in time. As I was creeping away, a car passed close by me. The passenger was a man wearing a cloak and a military cap. In the moonlight his eyes shone like emeralds. They seemed to be turned in my direction, and I shuddered. I knew it was *the Master*. You know what happened after that, Chi Foh."

"And I thank God it did happen, Moon Flower. But you're not really called Moon Flower, after all?"

Moon Flower drew closer to him. "Don't look so sad, dearest. I am. I was born on the night of a new moon and my, mother named me Jean Yueh Hua."

"Will you marry me on the next day there's a new moon?"

Moon Flower took his hand in both of hers.

"I'll marry you, Chi Foh—but on the first day my father is free again."

Dr. Fu-Manchu sat in his favorite chair behind the lacquered desk; it was early dawn. But only one lamp relieved the gloom, a green-shaded lamp on the desk which cast a phantom light over the yellow-robed figure. Fu-Manchu lay back, his elbows resting on the arms of the chair, the tips of his bony fingers pressed together, his eyes half closed, but glinting like emeralds where the light touched them.

In the shadowy room, two paces from the desk, the gigantic figure of Mahmud the Nubian stood motionless.

Fu-Manchu took a pinch of snuff from the silver snuffbox. He spoke softly.

"Go to your quarters, Mahmud, and remain there until further orders."

The big Nubian knelt on the rug, bent his head to the floor, stood up, made a deep salaam, and went out. He had a stealthy step, almost completely silent.

As he left by one door, another opened, and Huan Tsung-Chao came in. Fu-Manchu lay back in his chair, with closed eyes. General Huan settled himself upon the divan facing the desk.

"The man is honest and devoted," he said. "I have heard his account of all that happened, as you wished."

Fu-Manchu's eyes opened wide. They stared into the shadows from which Huan Tsung-Chao had spoken. "You heard how Skobolov, a dying man, tricked him in Niu-fo-tu and fled to some obscure resthouse? You heard how the Russian escaped again, taking his papers with him?"

He almost hissed the words, and then stood up, a tall, menacing figure.

"I heard, Master. I heard, also, that the escaped prisoner, Wu Chi Foh, was seen in Niu-fo-tu after Skobolov had arrived there."

"So the Si-Fan Register may now be on its way to Moscow."

"Or to London," came the placid reply from out of the shadows. "Sir Denis Nayland Smith is in China. A dying man is not hard to rob. And you suspected that the prisoner called Wu Chi Foh was working for British Intelligence in the first place."

Fu-Manchu dropped back in his chair.

"You know of my visit to Lao Tse-Mung. His behavior aroused deep suspicions. But he has the powers of a great diplomat. I have watched him for some years. Is he working with Nayland Smith? Is he opposed to Peiping? He remains impenetrable, and his estate is a fortress. To what party does he belong? These things we must find out, Tsung-Chao, or Lao Tse-Mung must be destroyed."

CHAPTER TWELVE

"This man, Skobolov," Nayland Smith snapped, "was one of the most trusted agents of the Kremlin." He raised his eyes from the documents found in the portfolio. "I know very little Russian, but enough to recognize his name as the person to whom these letters are addressed. This is very valuable evidence."

Tony nodded, smiling at Moon Flower.

"What I am anxious to know," Sir Denis added, "is what Skobolov was doing in Szechuan. Why was he sent here? It's a shot in the dark, but I venture to guess—*not this*."

He held up the bound manuscript written in Chinese.

"I agree with you, Sir Denis," Moon Flower said quietly. "I know written Chinese fairly well but this is in cipher and quite beyond me. Why should it be in cipher, if it weren't something highly secret?"

"Quite obvious, Jeanie. It can't be a top secret dispatch from Peiping. In the first place, it wouldn't be in Chinese; in the second, he would have headed for Russia and not come wandering around this remote province. Therefore, he must have acquired it in Szechuan."

He dropped the manuscript on the table and pulled at the lobe of his ear. "There are three people known to me who might decipher it. Lao Tse-Mung, his secretary, or our friend the lama in Niu-fo-tu. What's more, all of them speak Russian, and this correspondence interests me."

"Let us go to my uncle's," Moon Flower said eagerly. "We shall at least be safe while we're there, and Lao Tse-Mung's secretary is very clever, as you say, and knows many languages."

"You'd be safer still with your aunt in Hong Kong, young lady," Nayland Smith rapped.

Moon Flower smiled. "I shall never go back to Hong Kong until my father goes with me," she assured him. There was a convincing note of finality in the soft voice.

"You're going to be a big responsibility in the kind of work we have to do, Jeanie."

Moon Flower turned to Tony. "Was I a big responsibility to you, Chi Foh, in the kind of work we had to do?"

And honesty forced Tony to answer, "I couldn't have done it without you, Moon Flower."

Nayland Smith took his old briar pipe out of his pocket and began to refill the bowl. His expression was grim, but a smile lurked in his gray eyes.

"If McKay's against me, too, I suppose I must compromise. From the moment we leave this house we all carry our lives in our hands. We don't know what this Chinese manuscript is, but your account, McKay, of Skobolov's behavior and his strange death, tells us plainly that it's dynamite, and that *somebody* was following him to recover it. You agree?"

"I do, Sir Denis," Tony told him. "But if it was of such value to the Kremlin, it may be of equal value to us."

"If we can hang onto it," Nayland Smith snapped, "and not go the way of Skobolov."

There was a brief silence while he lighted his pipe.

"You have some theory about Skobolov?" Tony asked.

Nayland Smith nodded. "I have. He was poisoned. The mission of the poisoner was to recover this manuscript. I can think of only one man who is not only an expert poisoner but also a danger to the Soviet empire. Dr. Fu-Manchu."

Nayland Smith blew out a cloud of tobacco smoke.

"If I'm right, we have here the most powerful weapon against Fu-Manchu that I have ever held in my hands."

Many hours later, the security police held up an old Ford on a nearly impossible road some miles east of Lung Chang. The Chinese driver, whose shaved skull betrayed nothing but a stubble of hair, was a dull, taciturn fellow. His passengers were a lama, who wore glasses, and a Chinese boy.

The lama did the talking.

"Where did you come from and where are you going?" the man in charge wanted to know.

"From Yung Chuan," the Buddhist priest told him. "Are you a member of the faith, my son?"

"Never mind about that—"

"But it's more important than anything else."

"Who's the boy?"

"My pupil. I am returning to my monastery in Burma, and I am happy to say that I bring a young disciple with me."

The man, who evidently had special orders of some kind, looked from face to face.

"Who owns this car?"

"A good friend in Yung Chuan, and one of the faith. I have out-stayed my leave and am anxious to return."

"What's your friend's name?"

"Li Tao-shi. He has found the Path. Seek it, my son."

The man made a rude noise and waved the car on.

When they had gone a safe distance, the driver slowed down and turned a grinning face to his passengers.

"Good show, McKay!" he said. "You remembered your lines and never fluffed once. I don't know why those fellows were so alert, but it's just possible that the Master has sent out special orders. We're getting into the danger zone, now. Here's a crossroads. One way leads to a marsh as far as I can make out. Which way do we turn, Jeanie?"

The "disciple" hesitated. "I think we take the road to the marsh. Except in rainy weather it's quite passable. Then we should come to the main road to Lung Chang—if you think it's safe for us to use a main road."

"I don't. But is there any other way?"

"Not for a car. By water, yes. Otherwise, we have to walk."

Nayland Smith pulled reflectively at the lobe of his ear. "If we drive to the high road, how far is it from there to Lao Tse-Mung's house?"

"About five miles," Moon Flower answered.

"But from here, walking?"

"About the same, if I don't lose my way."

"Then, as two experienced pedestrians, I think you and McKay must walk. If stopped again, you know the story, McKay. Stick to it. We must separate for safety."

He raised the wizard walkie-talkie to his ear, adjusted it and listened, then. "Hullo, is that Sun Shao-Tung?" he said. "Yes. Nayland Smith here. Tell Lao Tse-Mung I have Yueh Hua and McKay with me. We're about five miles from the house and they are proceeding on foot. First, I must know if my Ford was noted by the Master when he arrived at the garage. It was? And what explanation was offered for its disappearance?" He listened attentively. "Ford used for collecting gardening material? Good. Had been sent into Chungking for repairs? Would be returned later by mechanic? Excellent. We'll be on our way." He turned to Tony.

"Did you follow, McKay?" he rapped.

"Yes, I did. Fu-Manchu has given orders for all ranks to look out for a Ford car. That's why we were held up. There must be more Fords in Szechuan than I suspected, or we shouldn't have slipped through so easily. You're right about breaking up the party, Sir Denis."

"I suspected this, McKay. I shall have to hang onto the briefcase. A missionary lama from Burma can't very well carry one. But, for safety, you take the Chinese manuscript."

The leather case was taken from its hiding place in the car and the mysterious manuscript tucked into a large pocket inside Tony's ample garment, which resembled a long-sleeved bathrobe.

When the parting took place, Moon Flower looked wistfully after the old Ford jolting away on the unpaved road. Tony knew what she was thinking and shared her feeling. Nayland Smith was an oasis in a desert, a well of resource. He put his arm around a slim waist concealed by the baggy boy's clothes.

"Come on, my lad," he said gaily, and kissed her. "We have faced worse things and survived."

Moon Flower clung to him, her blue eyes raised to his, and the blue eyes were somber.

"I am not afraid for us, Chi Foh," she assured him. "I am thinking about my father."

"We'll get him out, sweetheart. Don't doubt it."

"I don't dare to doubt it. But I feel, and you must feel, too, that this awful man, Dr. Fu-Manchu, is drawing a net around all of us. He has dreadful authority, and strange powers. I understand now that it was he who killed the Russian. But *how* did he kill him?"

"God knows! But it's pretty certain that his purpose was to get this thing I have in my pocket. For the moment, though, we're holding the cards."

"But he holds my father, a clever man and a man of strong character, helpless in his hands. Dr. Fu-Manchu is not an ordinary human being. He's a devil-inspired genius. Sir Denis is our only hope. And he has tried for years to conquer him. Alone, what could you and I do?"

Tony laughed, but not mirthfully. "Very little, I admit. Fu-Manchu has a vast underground organization behind him, and, at present anyway, the support of the government of China. We have nothing but our wits."

Moon Flower forced a smile. "Don't let me make you gloomy, Chi Foh. You mustn't pay too much attention to my moods. I don't expect us to overthrow Dr. Fu-Manchu. I only pray we may be able to get my father back alive."

Tony hugged her affectionately and kissed her hair, which she had cut short when Nayland Smith had decided that a lama priest couldn't travel in the company of a girl.

They set out on the path to Lung Chang.

It was a crazy path, bringing them through places along embankments crossing flooded paddy fields, and sometimes wandering among acres of opium poppies which had become a major crop since all restrictions had been removed. The collective authorities reaped a rich harvest from the sale of opium; the growers struggled to live.

The few peasants they met paid little attention to the lama priest and the boy who trudged on their way, except for one or two who were Buddhists. These respectfully saluted Tony, and he gave them a sign of hand which Nayland Smith had taught him.

They were in sight of a village which Moon Flower recognized, not more than a mile and a half from their destination, before anything disturbing happened. The day had been hot and they had pushed on at a good pace. They were tired. They had reached a point at which there was a choice of routes; they could either take the main road or a detour which would lengthen their journey.

"Should we risk the main road?" Tony asked. "Is it used much?"

"No," Moon Flower said. "But we would have to pass through the village. I think this is a county line, and there may be a police post there."

"Then I think we must go the long way, Moon Flower. Where will that lead us to?"

"To a gate in part of Lao Tse-Mung's property, nearly half a mile from the house. It is locked. But there's a hidden bell-push which rings a bell in the house. We have to cross the main road at one point, but the path continues on the other side."

"Then let's go."

They resumed their tramp. At a point where the path threatened to lose itself in a plantation of young bamboo, their luck deserted them. The thicket proved to border the road and as there was no sound of traffic they stepped out from the path onto a narrow, unpaved highway. And Moon Flower grasped Tony's arm.

A dusty bicycle lay on a bank, and sitting beside the cycle, smoking a cigarette, they saw a man in khaki police uniform.

Moon Flower suppressed a gasp. The policeman, however, looked more startled than they did as he got to his feet, dropping his

Chinese cigarette, which Tony knew from experience tasted like a firecracker. It was getting toward dusk and their sudden appearance out of the shadow bordering the road clearly had frightened him. The man grew very angry. He snatched up his cigarette.

"Where do you think you're going?" he demanded.

"We are trying to find our way to the river, which we have to cross. But we took the wrong path," Tony told him.

"And where are you going, then?"

"I have to return to my monastery in Burma. I am taking this young disciple with me."

"If you come from Burma, show me your papers, your permit to enter China."

Tony fumbled inside the loose robe. In an interior pocket he had all the necessary credentials which had been sent at top speed by Lao Tse-Mung to Chungking before the party set out, how obtained Tony could only guess. Lao Tse-Mung was a clever man.

He handed the little folder to the police officer, wondering if the man could read. Whether he could or not, evidently he recognized the official forms. They authorized the bearer to enter China and remain for thirty days. There was still a week to go. Tony wondered why the smoke of his cigarette, drooping from a corner of his coarse mouth, didn't suffocate him.

The man handed the passport back, clearly disappointed.

"Who is this boy?" he asked roughly. "Has he any official permit to travel?"

Thanks to Ray Jenkins, who had influential and corruptible friends in Chungking, "he" had. Tony produced a certificate for travel, signed by a member of the security bureau, authorizing Lo Hung-Chang, age 14, to leave his native town of Yung Chuan, but to report to security police at the Burma frontier before leaving China.

The disappointed policeman returned the certificate. Evidently he could read.

"You have only seven days to reach the frontier," he growled. "If it takes you any longer, look out for trouble."

"If I have earned this trouble, brother," Tony told him piously, "undoubtedly it will come to me, for my benefit. Have you not sought the Path?"

"*Your* path is straight ahead," the surly officer declared, furious because he had found nothing wrong. "You'll have to walk to Lung Chang and then on to Niu-fo-tu to reach the river." He dropped the last fragment of his stale cigarette and put his foot on it as Tony fumbled to return the certificate to his inside pocket. "You seem to have a lot of things in that pouch of yours. I have heard of lama priests getting away with pounds of opium that never saw the Customs. Turn out all you have there."

Tony's pulse galloped. He heard Moon Flower catch her breath. And he had to conquer a mad impulse to crush his fist into the face of the policeman. As he had done in jail at Chia-Ting, he reflected that Communist doctrines seemed to turn men into sadists. He hesitated. But only for a decimal of a second. He had money in a body belt, but carried nothing else, except the official papers which had been forged, and—the mystery manuscript.

He turned the big pocket out, handed the Chinese manuscript to the policeman.

If he attempted to confiscate it, Tony knew that no choice would be left. He would have to knock the man out before he had time to reach for the revolver which he carried. He watched him thumbing over the pages in fading light.

"What is this?" the policeman demanded.

Tony's breath returned to normal.

"A religious writing in the hand of a great disciple of our Lord Buddha. A present from this inspired scholar to my principal. If you could understand it, brother, you would already be on the Path."

"Brother" threw the manuscript down contemptuously. "Move on," he directed, and turned to his bicycle.

Moon Flower breathed a long sigh of relief as he rode off. "I wonder if you can imagine, Chi Foh," she said, "my feelings when you trusted that thing to him? I seemed to hear Sir Denis's words, 'the most powerful weapon against Fu-Manchu which I ever held in my hands.' Did you realize that he might have orders to look for it?"

"Yes. But the odds against it were heavy. And if he had tried anything, I was all set to make sure he didn't get away with it."

They reached their destination without further trouble and found Nayland Smith anxiously waiting for them.

CHAPTER THIRTEEN

For two days they remained in Lao Tse-Mung's house, apparently inactive, except that Nayland Smith spent hours alone, smoking pipe after pipe, deep in thought. Tony guessed that he was trying to discover a plan to rescue Dr. Cameron-Gordon and was finding it no easy thing to do.

With Moon Flower, Tony roamed about the beautiful gardens, and this brief interlude of peace was a chapter in his life which he knew he would always remember with happiness. Lao Tse-Mung had warned them all that Fu-Manchu was by no means satisfied with what he had seen and heard.

"My house will be watched. I shall be spied upon. If he discovers that you are here, none of us will be safe any longer. So never show yourselves at any point which is visible from the road. The entire property is walled, and the top of the walls are wired. But at places there are tall trees, which overlook the walls, and these trees I cannot wire."

Lao Tse-Mung's talented secretary, Sun Shao-Tung, had translated all the Russian letters in Skobolov's briefcase, and Nayland Smith had been interested to learn from the correspondence that the research scientist employed at the hidden Soviet plant was not a Russian, but a German, Dr. von Wehrner. But even more exciting was a penciled note which Sir Denis deduced to be a translation of a code message:

"If hidden Ms. as reported secure at any cost. Proceed as arranged to governor's villa to allay suspicion. Cancel further plans. Join plane at Huang-Ko-Shu."

"I was right, McKay," Nayland Smith declared. "This Chinese document is dynamite."

Sun Shao-Tung had gone to work on the mysterious manuscript. He had worked far into the night, only to find himself baffled.

Nayland Smith asked him to make a careful copy in case the original should be lost—or stolen. It was late during the second night of their stay at Lao Tse-Mung's house that something happened.

The secretary worked in a top room, equipped as an up-to-date office, with typewriter, filing cabinets, bookcases, and a large desk. This betrayed the modern side of the old mandarin, and was in keeping with his private airplane, his cars, his electrical lighting plant, and other equipment; a striking contrast to the Oriental character of the reception rooms below.

Tony occupied a room next to the office. Nayland Smith was lodged on the other side of the corridor. He was unaccountably restless. Lao Tse-Mung's guest rooms had electric lights and all the other facilities of a modem hotel. It was very late when Tony switched off his bedside lamp and tried to sleep. But the night seemed to be haunted by strange sounds, furtive movements which he couldn't identify or place.

The shadow of Fu-Manchu was creeping over him. He began thinking, again, about the dead Russian, seeing in his imagination the man's ceaseless battle with clouds of invisible insects. Of course, it had been delirium. But what a queer kind of delirium. Skobolov had died at the hand of Dr. Fu-Manchu. But of *what* had he died?

Tony found himself listening intently for a buzz of insects in the room.

He heard none. He tried to laugh at these phantom fears.

Then he began to listen again.

There *was* a sound—a very faint sound. It was not a sound of insects, and it was not in his room. It came from the adjoining office.

He knew that Sun Shao-Tung had retired two hours before. He had heard him go. Yet something or someone moved in the office.

Tony swung out of bed, stole to the door of his room, opened it cautiously.

Barefooted, he crept along to the office door.

He stood listening, silently.

Yes, there was someone inside!

He began to turn the handle and gently opened the door. As it opened, a draft of cold air swept onto his face.

It brought with it a sense of horror. He shuddered, then fully opened the door.

The office was in darkness. But a beam of moonlight through the open window just brushed the top of the large desk. There was a dim figure in the shadow behind the desk, and two hands, which alone were visible in the moonlight, busily swept up a litter of papers lying there.

Perhaps the lighting created an illusion. *But they were gray hands!*

Tony clenched his fists, took a step forward, and a lean figure sprang over the desk, leapt upon him, and had his throat in an icy grip.

He uttered a stifled shriek as that ghastly grip closed on him; it was a cry of loathing rather than fear. But in the face of what he knew to be deadly peril, his brain remained clear. He struck a right, a left to the jaw of his antagonist. The blows registered. The grip on his throat relaxed. He struck again. But he was becoming dizzy.

Desperately, he threw himself on the vaguely outlined figure that was strangling him. He touched the naked body—and the body was *cold.*

He was fighting with a living corpse!

Very near the end of his resources, he used his knee viciously. The thing grunted, fell back, and sprang toward the open window.

Swaying like a drunken man, he saw, dimly, a gray figure sweep up something from the desk and leap to the window. Tony tottered, threw out his arms to save himself, and collapsed on the floor. His outstretched hands touched a heavy bronze bowl which the secretary used as a wastebasket.

Pain, anger, gave him a brief renewal of strength. He grasped the bowl, forced himself to his feet, and hurled the bowl at the head of the retreating thing.

It reached its target. He heard the dull thud. It rebounded and crashed against the glass of the opened window.

But the living-dead horror vanished.

Lights... voices... arms which lifted him... the tang of brandy.

Tony came to life.

The lighted office looked red. His head swam. Through this red mist he saw Nayland Smith bending over him.

"A close call, McKay. Take it easy."

Tony found himself in a deep rest-chair. He had some difficulty in swallowing. He managed to sit up.

"It went through the window," he croaked hoarsely, "although… I hit it on the head with… that."

The bronze bowl lay among a litter of glass.

"I know," Sir Denis snapped. "It's phenomenal. We have search parties out."

"But—"

"Don't strain your throat, McKay. Yes. It has the cipher manuscript."

In Lao Tse-Mung's library, surrounded by an imposing collection of books in many languages, four men assembled. A servant placed a variety of refreshments on a low table around which they sat, and was dismissed. The staff's quarters were separated from the house, and the disturbance in the office had not reached them. Mercifully, it had failed to arouse Moon Flower, whose apartment was in the west wing. The thing which had happened in the night was known only to these four who met in the library.

Lao Tse-Mung and his frightened secretary sipped tea. Tony and Nayland Smith drank Scotch and soda. Tony smoked a cigarette and Sir Denis smoked his pipe.

"My chief mechanic reports," their host stated in his calm voice and perfect English, "that the connections are undisturbed. Six men are now examining the possible points of entry, and if anything is discovered to account for the presence of this thief in my house, I shall be notified immediately."

"When it's daylight," Nayland Smith said, "I'll take a look, myself."

"Of course you understand, Sir Denis, what has happened? We have had a visit from a Cold Man. These creatures have been reported in the neighborhood of Chia-Ting on more than one occasion, but never here. It is a punishable offense to touch them. If seen, the police must be informed. An ambulance from a hospital established recently in that area by the governor, Huan Tsung-Chao, is soon on the scene, I understand; the attendants seem to know how to deal with these ghastly phenomena. They are believed, by the ignorant people, to be vampires and are known as 'the living-dead.'"

"The ignorant people have my sympathy," Tony declared hoarsely.

"Personally," Nayland Smith snapped, "I'm not surprised. That master of craft, Dr. Fu-Manchu, has discovered that I am here. That it was he who murdered Skobolov in order to recover this manuscript is beyond dispute. But how he found out that it had fallen into *my* hands is a mystery."

"I warned you," Lao Tse-Mung pointed out in his quiet way, "that my house would be watched."

"You did," Nayland Smith agreed, bitterly. "But even so, how did the watcher discover the very room in which this manuscript lay? And, crowning mystery, how did the Cold Man get in to steal it?"

As he ceased speaking, the large room seemed to become eerily still. This stillness was broken by a sound which sent a chill through Tony's nerves. Although a long way off, it was as clearly audible, penetrating, and horrifying as the wail of a banshee. A long minor cry, rising to a high final note on which it died away.

Even Lao Tse-Mung clutched the arms of his chair. Nayland Smith sprang up as if electrified.

"You heard it, McKay?"

"Of course I heard it. For God's sake, what was it?"

"A sound I haven't heard for years and never expected to hear in China. It was the warning cry of a dacoit. Fu-Manchu has always employed these Burmese robbers and assassins. Come on, McKay! I have a revolver in my pocket. Are you armed?"

"No."

"You may have my gun," Lao Tse-Mung volunteered, entirely restored to his normal calm. From under his robe he produced a small but serviceable automatic. "It is fully charged. What do you propose to do, Sir Denis?"

"To try to find the spot where that call came from."

Nayland Smith was heading for the door when a faint bell-note detained him.

"Wait," Lao Tse-Mung directed.

The old mandarin drew back the loose sleeve of his robe. Tony saw that he wore one of the phenomenal two-way radios on his wrist. He listened, spoke briefly, then disconnected.

"My chief mechanic reports, Sir Denis, that the cry we heard came from a point between the main gate and the drive-in to the garage. He is there now."

"Come on, McKay," Nayland Smith repeated, and ran out, followed by Tony.

They headed for the main gate, looking grotesque in their pajamas and robes. They slowed down as they reached the gate, stood still, and listened. The sound of voices reached them from somewhere ahead.

Tony found himself retracing that sloping path behind the high wall which led to the garage—the path along which Mai Cha had taken him on the memorable night he had escaped the Master.

The beam of a flashlight presently led them to Lao Tse-Mung's chief mechanic. He had two other men with him. A tall ladder was propped against the wall, and another man could be seen on the top looking over. Sir Denis was expected, for Wong, the mechanic, saluted and reported. He spoke Chinese with a Szechuan dialect which seemed to puzzle Sir Denis but with which Tony's travels in the area had made him fairly familiar. Fortunately, he also spoke quite good English.

He had been walking toward this point, scanning the parapet of the wall with his flashlight, when that awful cry broke the silence, and died away. "It came from about here," Wong said. "I called out, and the nearest man in the search party ran to join me. My orders were not to open the gates and not to disconnect the wiring. The gardeners brought a ladder so that we could look into the road. It is set so that the rungs do not touch the wires. But the man up there can see nothing and I have ordered him to come down."

"You have heard no other sound?" Tony asked him.

"Not a movement," the man assured him. "Nothing stirred."

The gardener descended from the long ladder and was about to remove it.

"One moment," Nayland Smith snapped. "I want to take a look. This intrigues me."

"Be careful of the wiring," Wong warned. "It carries a high voltage and a slight touch is enough."

"*That* wouldn't interest you," Tony called out as Nayland Smith started up the ladder.

"That's just what *does* interest me!" Sir Denis called back.

He mounted right to the top of the ladder. He didn't look out onto the road; he looked fixedly at the parapet where the wires were stretched. Then he came down. From a pocket of his gown he took his pipe and his pouch.

"There are two other things I must know, McKay. For one of them we have to wait for daylight. The other it's just possible we might find tonight." He turned to Wong. "Take the ladder away. I'm glad you brought it."

He grasped Tony's arm. "I have a flashlight in my pocket. Walk slowly back to the house, not by the route we came, but by the nearest way to the windows of your room and the office."

As they started, Nayland Smith, pipe in mouth, kept flashing light into shadowy shrubberies which bordered the path.

"I don't know what you're looking for," Tony declared.

"I may be wrong, McKay. It's no more than what you call a hunch. But I do know what I'm looking for. It's a hundred to one chance and if I'm wrong I'll tell you. If I'm right, you'll see for yourself."

They walked slowly on. There was little breeze. Sometimes the flashlight brought about a queer rustling in the shrubberies as of some sleeping creatures disturbed or nocturnal things scuffling to shelter. In the light of a declining moon, bats could be seen swooping silently overhead.

His gruesome experience with a Cold Man vividly in mind, Tony found himself threatened, as they moved slowly along, by a shapeless terror. Partly, it was a creation of the dark and stillness, an upsurge of hereditary superstition. Things he couldn't explain had happened. At any moment, he thought, icy fingers might clutch his throat again. Of human enemies he had no fear. But what were these Cold Men? Were they human, or were they, as some who had seen them believed, animated dead men, zombies?

Nayland Smith worked diligently, yard by yard.

He found nothing.

And Tony knew, by observing the furious way in which he puffed at his pipe, that he was disappointed.

They had reached the gate lodge, which was in darkness, and had turned left, instead of to the right which was the way they had come, before Sir Denis uttered a word.

Then he said rapidly, "Here's our last chance."

They were in a narrow, little-used path, overgrown by wild flowers. It led to the east wing of the house, but not to any entrance. It would, though, as Tony realized, lead them to a point directly below the window of his own room and that of the office.

Tirelessly, Nayland Smith explored every shadow with his flashlight, but found nothing until, in a clump of tangled undergrowth surrounding a tall tulip tree, he pulled up.

"I was right!"

The ray of the lamp lighted a grisly spectacle.

A man lay there, a man whose body was gray, whose only clothing consisted of a loin cloth, and this was gray, and a tightly knotted gray turban. He lay in a contorted attitude, his head twisted half under his body.

"This is what I was looking for," Nayland Smith said. "Look. His neck's broken."

"Good God! Is this—"

"The Cold Man who attacked you? Yes. And you killed him."

Tony stood, hands clenched, looking at the ghastly thing under the tulip tree. Suddenly in that warm night, he felt chilled...

"The first specimen," Nayland Smith stated grimly, "to fall into my hands. Rumor hasn't exaggerated. I can feel the chill even here." He stepped forward.

"Careful, Sir Denis."

Nayland Smith turned. "The poor devil's harmless now, McKay. He's out of the clutches of Dr. Fu-Manchu at last. Some day, I hope, we shall know how these horrors are created. His skin is an unnatural gray, but I recognize the features. The man is Burmese." He stooped over the contorted body. "Hullo! Thank heaven, McKay, the hundred to one chance has come off."

From the gray loincloth he dragged out a bundle of papers, shone the ray of the lamp on it, and sprang upright so excitedly that he dropped his pipe.

"Sun Shao-Tung's notes and the Chinese manuscript. Our luck's changed, McKay." He picked up his pipe. "Let me show you something." He stooped again, lighted the face of the Cold Man. "Contrary to official belief, dacoity, thought to be extinct, is a religious cult. Look."

He tore the gray turban from the dead man's head. Tony drew nearer.

"What, Sir Denis?"

The flashlight was directed on the shaven head.

"The caste mark."

Tony looked closely. Just above the line of the turban he saw a curious mark, either tattooed or burnt onto the skin.

"A dacoit," Nayland Smith told him.

"Then it was he who gave that awful moaning cry?"

"No," Sir Denis replied. "That was my hunch. It was *another* dacoit who gave the cry."

CHAPTER FOURTEEN

Three times Matsukata, the Japanese physician in charge of the neighboring clinic, had come into a small room attached to Dr. Fu-Manchu's laboratory in which the doctor often rested and sometimes, when he had worked late, slept. It was very simply equipped, the chief item of furniture being a large, cushioned divan.

A green-shaded lamp stood on a table littered with papers and books, and its subdued light provided the sole illumination. The air was polluted with sickly fumes of opium.

Dr. Fu-Manchu lay on the divan entirely without movement. Even his breathing was not perceptible. A case of beautifully fashioned opium pipes rested on a small table beside him, with a spirit lamp, a jar of the purest *chandu,* and several silver bodkins. In spirit, Dr. Fu-Manchu was far from the world of ordinary men, and his body rested; perhaps the only real rest he ever knew.

Matsukata stood there, silent, watching, listening. Then, once more he withdrew.

Quite a few minutes had passed in the silent room when Fu-Manchu raised heavy lids and looked around. The green eyes were misty, the pupils mere pinpoints. But as he sat up, by some supreme command of his will, the mist cleared, the contracted pupils enlarged. He used opium as he used men, for his own purpose; but no man and no drug was his master.

It was his custom, in those periods of waiting for a fateful decision, which the average man spends in pacing the floor, checking each passing minute, to smoke a pipe of *chandu* and so enter that enchanted realm to which opium holds the key.

But now he was instantly alert, in complete command of all his faculties. He struck a small gong on the table beside him.

Matsukata came in before the vibration of the gong had ceased.

"Well?" Fu-Manchu demanded.

Matsukata bowed humbly. "I regret to report failure, Master."

Fu-Manchu clenched his hands. "You mean that Singu failed?"

"Singu failed to return, Master."

"But Singu was a Cold Man, a mere automaton under your direction," Fu-Manchu spoke softly. "If anything failed, Matsukata, it was your direction."

"That is not so, Master. Something unforeseen occurred. Where, I cannot tell. But when more than ten minutes past his allotted time had elapsed, Ok, who was watching from the point of entry, reported a man with a flashlight approaching. I ordered Ok to give the warning to which Singu should have replied. There was no reply. I ordered Ok to remove evidence of our mode of entry. It was just in time. A party of men was searching the grounds."

Dr. Fu-Manchu stood up slowly. He folded his arms.

"Is that all your news?" he asked in a whisper. "The Si-Fan Register is lost?"

"That is all, Master."

"You may go. Await other orders."

Matsukata bowed deeply, and went out.

In Lao Tse-Mung's library, Nayland Smith was speaking. Gray, ghostly daylight peered in at the windows.

"Dacoits never work alone. During my official years in Burma I furnished reports to London which proved, conclusively, that dacoity was not dead. I also discovered that, like thuggee, it was not merely made up of individual gangs of hoodlums, but was a religious cult. Dr. Fu-Manchu, many years ago, obtained absolute control of the dacoits. He even has a bodyguard of dacoits. Probably the Cold Man, who lies dead out there, was formerly one of them."

Lao Tse-Mung's alert, wrinkle-framed eyes were fixed upon Sir Denis. Tony chainsmoked.

"Of the powers of these creatures, called, locally, Cold Men, we know nothing. But we do know, now, that they are—or were— normal human beings. By some hellish means they have been converted to this form. But certainly their powers are supernormal and the temperature of their bodies is phenomenal; they are cold as blocks of ice."

Tony found himself shivering. His first encounter with a Cold Man had made an impression that would last forever.

"How you got onto the fact that he was lying somewhere on that path is beyond me," he declared.

"It was a theory, McKay, based on experience. Whenever I have heard that call it has always been a warning to one dacoit who was operating, from another who was watching. Since it's getting light now, I hope to find out shortly how the Cold Man got into the grounds."

"But how did he get into the office?"

"That," Nayland Smith answered, "is not so difficult. There is a tall tulip tree growing close to the house some twenty yards from the window. These Burmese experts often operate from the roof. Evidently, even when changed to Cold Men, they retain these acrobatic powers.

"It's likely that he lowered himself from the roof to enter the room and returned to the roof to make his escape. But your lucky shot with the metal bowl registered." He turned to Tony. "It would have killed a normal man. It only dazed the dacoit. He got back as far as the tall tulip tree, sprang to a high branch—and missed it."

Sir Denis knocked ashes from his pipe and began to reload the charred bowl.

"Your analysis of the night's events," came Lao Tse-Mung's mellow voice, "is entirely logical. But there's one mystery which you have not cleared up. I refer to the fact that those who instructed this man must have known that the document in cipher was here."

Nayland Smith paused in the act of pressing the tobacco into the bowl of his pipe.

"I don't think they *knew* it," he replied thoughtfully. "But since McKay was identified in Niu-fo-tu as the escaped prisoner, and the dying Skobolov was in the neighborhood at the same time, Fu-Manchu may have surmised that McKay had gotten possession of the document and brought it to me."

In the early morning, a party of frightened and shivering men under Nayland Smith's direction carried a long, heavy wooden box out from the main gate and across the narrow road. In a cypress wood bordering the road they dug a deep grave, and buried the Cold Man.

The body remained supernaturally chilled.

Sir Denis, having dismissed the burial party, set off with Tony at a rapid pace in the direction of the main gate. Soon they reached the spot where the gardeners had placed the ladder that night. Nayland Smith quickly identified it by marks on the soil where it had rested. Then, foot by foot, he examined every inch of ground under the wall for several yards east and west of it.

At last he cried triumphantly, "Look!" and pointed down. "Just as I thought!"

Tony looked. He saw two narrow holes in the earth, which looked as if they'd been made by the penetration of a walking stick.

"What does this mean?"

"It means what I suspected, McKay. I have the key to the main gate. Here it is. Go out and walk back along the road. I'll sing out to guide you. When you get to the spot where I'm standing, inside, look for similar marks, outside."

Tony took the key and ran to the gate. He unlocked it and began to do as Nayland Smith had directed. When he reached a point which he judged was near where Sir Denis waited, he called out.

"Three paces more," came the crisp reply.

He took three paces. "Here I am."

"Search."

Tony found the job no easy one. Coarse grass and weeds grew beside the road close up to the wall. But, persevering, he noticed a patch which seemed to have been trodden down. He stooped, parted the tangled undergrowth with his fingers, and at last found what he was looking for: two identical holes in the earth.

"Found 'em?" Nayland Smith called from the other side of the wall.

"Yes, Sir Denis. They're here!"

"Come back, and relock the gate."

Tony obeyed, rejoined Nayland Smith. "What does all this mean?"

Sir Denis grinned impishly. "It means two light bamboo ladders, long enough to clear the wiring and meeting above it on top. It's as simple as that."

Tony gaped for a moment; then he began to laugh. "So much for Lao Tse-Mung's fortress!"

"Quite so," Nayland Smith spoke grimly. "It could be entered by an agile man using only one ladder. Now, to find the last piece of evidence on which my analysis of this business rests. I have examined the wall below the office window, and no one could reach the window from the ground. Therefore, it's certain that he reached it from the roof as I suspected last night."

They returned to the house, where Wong was waiting for them.

"The trap to the roof," he reported, "is above the landing of the east wing. I have had a step ladder put there and have unbolted the trap."

"Good." Nayland Smith lighted his pipe. "Show the way."

Wong ducked his head, stepped into the narrow, V-shaped closet, reached up, and opened a trap. A shaft of daylight appeared in the opening.

"Wait until I'm up, McKay," Sir Denis directed. "Then follow on. Four eyes are better than two."

He raised his arms, wedged his foot on a projection, and was gone. Tony followed and found himself lying at the base of the curved Chinese roof, and only prevented from falling off by the curl of the highly decorated edge. Nayland Smith, on all fours, was already crawling along the ledge. Tony glanced over the side and saw at a glance that they were no more than a few yards from the office and his own room below.

As this fact dawned upon him, Nayland Smith turned his head and looked back.

"I was right," he cried. "Here's what I was looking for."

He held up a length of shiny, thin rope. One end apparently was fastened to an ornament on the curling lip of the roof.

Tony turned cautiously and crawled back. He saw, when Sir Denis joined him, that he carried the coil of rope. But it was not until they were in Tony's room that he explained what, already, was fairly clear. He held up the thin line.

"Notice," he said, "that it's knotted at intervals. It's a silk rope and strong as a cable. You saw that it was fastened to one of the gargoyles decorating the edge of the roof. A dacoit's rope. I have seen many. His weight, as he first swung down to the window and then hauled himself up again, so tightened the knot that he couldn't get it free when he returned to the roof. He dared not wait. He ran along the roof to the tulip tree—and broke his neck."

CHAPTER FIFTEEN

That night a counsel of war was held. "Whatever information he may have," Lao Tse-Mung stated, "the Master dare not take active steps against me. It is clear that we hold a document which is of vital importance to him. This is my shield. Your presence, Sir Denis, requires no explanation, nor does that of Moon Flower. But you, Captain McKay, as a secret agent once under arrest, pose a problem."

"I quite agree, sir," Tony admitted.

"What are we going to do?" Moon Flower asked, her blue eyes anxious. "Even if Fu-Manchu does not have you arrested, Sir Denis has told you that his awful servants, the Cold Men, can get in almost any night."

Lao Tse-Mung smiled in his gentle way.

"For a few more nights, possibly, Moon Flower. And I have arranged a patrol of the walls which will make even this difficult. Then, advised by Sir Denis, and in conference with my engineers, I have prepared a surprise for invaders."

"It boils down to this," Nayland Smith announced. "We're all three going to move, tonight. We meet at the house of the lama,

Dr. Li Wu Chang, in Niu-fo-tu. I could discard disguise and travel openly, as I'm entitled to do, taking Jeanie with me. Fu-Manchu knows I'm in Szechuan, although I'm uncertain how he found out. It's open warfare. But in view of all we have to do, this would be to play into Fu-Manchu's hands. He must be made to believe that I have returned to Hong Kong. Our good friend, Lao Tse-Mung, has undertaken this part of the scheme, and his private plane will leave for Hong Kong tonight."

"But you won't be on board?" Tony asked.

"I shall be on my way to Niu-fo-tu. I shall take over the part of the Burmese monk retiring to his monastery with a young disciple. Our host has provided me with suitable papers. Hang onto those you have. You, also, must travel as a Buddhist priest. You know your own story, your name, and the name of your monastery. The travel permit for the disciple I must have."

"All clear."

"We'll set out together, in the old Ford, until I say 'Beat it.' Then you'll leave and be on your own."

"Agreed," Tony said.

"Leave the details to me. Yours may be the harder part, McKay, but you're used to the hard way. Jeanie insists on joining us, so let it go at that. We start at nine sharp."

On a long cane settee outside the library, where flowering vines laced the terrace, and the gardens under a crescent moon looked like fairyland, Tony and Moon Flower continued the conference.

"Yueh Hua," he whispered, "why must you come with us? God knows I always want you near me, but we're up against enemies who stop at nothing. Dr. Fu-Manchu uses strange methods. These Cold Men! Couldn't you stay right here, where you're safe, until a better time comes to join me?"

He could feel her heart beating against his own when she answered.

"No, Chi Foh. I know Sir Denis has some plan to release my father, and I may be part of it. I can't be wrong because otherwise I'm sure he would have told me to stay."

Tony held her close. "When Sir Denis needs you he will send for you."

"He needs me now, or he wouldn't take me. Don't worry about me, Chi Foh. It is *you* I'm worrying about. If we have to separate, and someone recognizes you as an escaped prisoner—"

"The odds are against it. I know enough about the game, now, to take care of myself. I have credentials, too, and I'll get by."

The rest of the conference had no bearing on the problem.

There was a fairly good road, as Chinese roads go, to Niu-fo-tu, as Tony remembered. And when they set out, Nayland Smith driving, Moon Flower beside him, and Tony in the back, moonlight was adequate to prevent a driver from coming to grief on the many obstacles met with.

Nayland Smith was an expert driver, but his speed on this unpredictable surface was scarcely relaxing. There was no great distance to go, and he took bends with a confidence that showed he meant to get there in the shortest possible time.

"I'm afraid, Jeanie," Tony heard him say, "my many journeys in Scotland Yard days with the Flying Squad have taught me bad manners."

His remarkable driving got them to within sight of the dim lights which indicated the market town of Niu-fo-tu, a place of unhappy memory.

Suddenly these dim lights were reinforced by a red light.

"Beat it, McKay!" Nayland Smith ordered and checked down. "Make a detour. You know something of the lay of the land. Head for the lama's back door. If picked up, do your stuff. Admit that's where you're going. You're fellow Buddhists."

Tony jumped out. He had a glimpse of Moon Flower looking back; then he made his way to the roadside, tried to recall what he knew of the immediate neighborhood, and groped a way through a bamboo jungle to a spot where he could sit down.

He had a packet of cigarettes and a lighter in the pocket of his ungainly robe. He took them out, lighted a cigarette, and sat down to consider his next move.

Which side was the river? If he could mentally locate the spot where the sampan had been tied up, he could work out his route to the path which would lead him to the back door of the lama's house.

From his cover, he watched the Ford pass out of sight.

He was alone again. He must act alone.

A few minutes' reflection convinced him that the Lu Ho River lay on his left. He must follow the road as closely as possible to the outskirts of the town. Then he must bear north-westerly, if he could find a path, and this would bring him to the open country behind the lama's house.

Without further delay, he returned to the road and started walking.

What was Nayland Smith's plan? That he had one seemed evident, since he was re-entering the danger zone. Tony's heart sank when he reflected that he had rescued Moon Flower from the clutches of Fu-Manchu and that now she was venturing again into his reach. But he loved her loyalty, her fighting spirit which made her ready to defy even such an enemy as Dr. Fu-Manchu.

He strode along confidently until he had a distant view of the gate of the town, but not the gate by which he had entered on a previous occasion. He pulled up, made a swift mental calculation, and got his bearings.

As he stepped aside from the high road into a tangle of bushes, a heavy wagon of market produce lumbered along, and from his cover he saw, again, the red light spring up ahead.

Evidently, there was a guard at the gate. What was the reason for these unusual precautions? And how had Nayland Smith been received?

Anxiety surged up in him like a hot spring.

He peered out. The big cart was being detained. He saw a number of men around it. He moved on. Still keeping parallel with the road, he tried to find some sort of path leading in the direction he wanted to go.

And soon he found one.

It was a footpath from the high road, bearing north-westerly, just such a path as he had hoped to find. He sighed with relief; began to trudge along.

But fifty yards from the road, he stopped. His heart seemed to stop, too.

The Ford stood beside the narrow footpath.

He sprang forward. The car was empty. It had been deserted.

His brain began to behave like a windmill, and he broke into a run. What did it mean? What had happened? This was the car Nayland Smith had been driving. Where was Nayland Smith—and where was Moon Flower?

The path led into a patch of dense shadow, deserted by moonlight. He ran on.

A steely grasp on his ankle! He was thrown, pinned down.

Tony twisted, threw off his unseen enemy, nearly got onto his knees, when a strangle-hold ended the struggle.

"The light—quick!" came a snappy command.

A light flashed dazzlingly onto Tony's face.

"Chi Foh!" Moon Flower's voice.

"Damn it, McKay. I'm awfully sorry."

He had been captured by Nayland Smith.

"I thought we had been spotted," Sir Denis explained. "Hearing someone apparently in pursuit, I naturally acted promptly."

"You certainly did," Tony admitted. "I'm getting quite used to being strangled."

"You see, McKay, in sight of the town gate, I saw a loaded cart being examined; several lanterns were brought out. I recognized one of the searchers—the big Nubian. That settled it. I looked for an opening where I could turn in, scrapped the old Ford, and went ahead on foot."

"I understand. I did the same thing; and I think, but I'm not sure, that we have picked the right path. If so, we haven't far to walk. But what's going on in Niu-fo-tu? Is Fu-Manchu expecting us?"

They were walking ahead cautiously, speaking in low tones.

"That's what bothers me," Nayland Smith confessed. "I don't understand it."

Moon Flower had said little for some time, but now she broke her silence. "As we have the mysterious manuscript, surely Fu-Manchu would expect us to get away and not to come back here."

"I agree," Sir Denis said. "There may be some other reason for these strange precautions."

They came out from the shadow of trees. The path led sharply right, and they saw the scattered houses of Niu-fo-tu, silvered by moonlight. The house of the lama, Dr. Li Wu Chang, was easy to identify, and Tony recognized the door by which he had escaped.

"Is the lama expecting us?" he asked Nayland Smith.

"Yes. He has been advised. Hurry. We can be seen from several points now."

In less than two minutes they were at the door. It was a teak door with a grille. It was locked.

Nayland Smith fumbled about urgently and presently found what he was looking for. A faint bell-note sounded inside the house.

"I think someone is coming along this way," Moon Flower whispered. "Perhaps we have been seen."

The grille opened. There was a face outlined behind the bars.

"Nayland Smith," Sir Denis said.

The door was opened. They hurried in, and the old woman who had opened the door closed and barred it.

At that moment the lama came out of his study, hands extended.

"You are welcome. I was growing anxious. My sister, who looks after me, will take charge of Miss Cameron-Gordon, and presently we will all share a frugal supper."

Later in the lama's study, with its churchlike smell, and refreshed by a bottle of excellent wine, their host told them an astonishing thing.

"I received a message from Lao Tse-Mung who called to learn if you had arrived. It seems that a Cold Man entered his house to steal a valuable document but that the attempt was frustrated and the creature killed?"

"Correct," Nayland Smith agreed. "He was also buried."

"So I understand, Sir Denis. Lao Tse-Mung informs me that his chief mechanic, a very faithful and intelligent servant, reported to him shortly after you had departed that he had heard voices and strange sounds from the cypress grove in which the burial had taken place. He asked for permission to investigate. It was granted."

"Wong's a good man," Nayland Smith said, his gray eyes brightening. "I don't know another among all of them that would go near that grave at night. What did he find?"

"He found the grave reopened, and empty."

A blue light went out in the small cabinet which faced Dr. Fu-Manchu. He glanced across at General Huan who sat watching him.

"Mahmud reports that the consignment from Lung Chang has passed through Niu-fo-tu. On the outskirts of the town it will be transferred to the motor wagon and should be here very shortly."

General Huan took a pinch of snuff. "In my ignorance, Master, it seems to me that to employ your great powers upon a matter which cannot advance our cause..."

Fu-Manchu raised his hand, stood up slowly. His eyes became fixed in an almost maniacal stare, his fingers seemed to quiver.

"Cannot advance our cause?" The words were hissed. "How do you suppose, Tsung-Chao, that I have been able to accomplish even so little? Is it because I am a master politician? No. Because I am a great soldier? No. Why do I stand before you, alive? Because I was chosen by the gods to outlive my normal span of years? *No!*"

His voice rose to a guttural cry. He clenched his hands.

"I regret my clumsy words, Master. I would have said..."

"You would have spoken folly. It is because I have explored more secrets of nature than any man living today. The fools who send rockets into space—what cause do these toys advance? I constructed a machine thirty years ago which defies the law of gravity. What of those who devise missiles with destructive warheads to reach distant targets? I could erase human life from the face of the earth without employing such a clumsy device." Fu-Manchu dropped back into his chair, breathing heavily.

"Forgive me. I had no wish to disturb you."

"I am not disturbed, Tsung-Chao. I am disappointed to find that our long association has not shown you that it is my supremacy as a scientist which alone can carry our projects to success. And what is my greatest achievement to this present hour? The creation of the Cold Men. You may not know, therefore I tell you that the Cold Men are *dead men.*"

Huan Tsung-Chao stirred uneasily, looked aside.

"You are startled. Matsukata alone knew the secret, which now you share. Every one of the Cold Men has died, or has been put to death, and from the cold ashes I have recreated the flame of life. None, save Singu, has ever been buried as dead. For a man once dead cannot die a second time."

General Huan's masklike features relaxed into an expression which almost resembled one of fear.

"I am appalled, Master. Forgive my ignorance, but Matsukata reported that Singu died of a broken neck."

Dr. Fu-Manchu laughed harshly. "He reported that Singu had suffered a dislocation of the anterior ligament as the result of a fall on his head. There were other injuries to the skull which may indicate the cause of this fall. The ligament I can repair; the other injury also."

"But…"

"But if I cannot restore Singu to life, long years of research will have led me to a hollow fallacy. I believed the Cold Men to be indestructible except by total disintegration."

There was a faint sound, and Fu-Manchu turned a switch. The voice of the Japanese physician, Matsukata, was heard faintly.

"I have the body in the clinic, Master."

"Do nothing until I join you."

Dr. Fu-Manchu stood up. "Would you care to witness one of the most important experiments I have ever carried out, Tsung-Chao?"

"Thank you, no," the old soldier replied. "I fear no living man; but dead men who walk again turn my old blood to water."

CHAPTER SIXTEEN

Tony stared out of a window into one of the busiest streets of Chia-Ting. This was part of the city he had never previously visited. His knowledge of Chia-Ting was confined to the waterfront and the jail. Accompanied by the old lama, whose credentials were above suspicion, they had made the journey of approximately thirty miles without incident, as members of his family bound for Chungtu.

Nayland Smith and Tony had adopted the dress of members of the professional class, and Moon Flower was a girl again—Sir Denis's daughter. The house in Chia-Ting belonged to a cousin of the lama, a prosperous physician and a fervent anti-Communist.

But this evening, Tony was worried.

Nayland Smith and his "daughter" had traced, at last, the house in which Shun-Hi, former servant of Dr. Cameron-Gordon, was living. Moon Flower's memory of its location was rather hazy. They had gone to interview Shun-Hi.

And although dusk was near, they had not returned.

Sir Denis had insisted that until the time for action came, Tony must not show himself unnecessarily in Chia-Ting. Too many people knew him, and the reward for his arrest would stimulate recognition.

He still had little more than a vague idea of Nayland Smith's plan. That the girl, Shun-Hi, was a link with Moon Flower's father he saw clearly. But he saw no connection, whatever, between this visit and Dr. Cameron-Gordon's release from Dr. Fu-Manchu. But if anyone could free the imprisoned scientist, Nayland Smith was the man.

Just before his anxiety became unendurable, Tony saw Moon Flower and Sir Denis making for the door below. They had a girl with them whom he guessed to be Shun-Hi, and a few moments later all three came into the room.

Nayland Smith looked elated. "Our luck holds, McKay. Here's a useful recruit. Sit down, Shun-Hi. We have a lot to talk about."

Shun-Hi, a good-looking working-class girl, smiled happily at Moon Flower and sat down. Moon Flower sat beside her, an encouraging arm thrown around Shun-Hi's shoulders, as Nayland Smith began to fill his pipe.

"Is your father well, Yueh Hua?" Tony asked.

Moon Flower nodded. "Yes, but desperately unhappy."

"Shun-Hi," Sir Denis explained, "speaks remarkably good English. So now, Shun-Hi, I want to ask you some questions. You tell me that your old employer, the doctor, works in a laboratory in the garden but sleeps in the house. How large is this laboratory?"

"It is..." Shun-Hi hesitated... "like four of this room in a row... so." She extended her hands.

"A long, low building. I see. And where's the door?"

"One at each end. From the door at the far end there is a path to a gate. But the gate is always locked."

"And inside?"

"No one is allowed inside. Sometimes, I carry a tray down for the doctor. His lunch. But I put it on the ledge of a window and he takes

144

it in. This was how I got Miss Yueh Hua's message to him and got his reply back."

"Does he work alone there?"

"Yes. Except when a Japanese from the hospital comes, or when the Master is there. The Master spends many hours inside this place."

"And when the window is opened, what can you see?"

"Only a very small room, with a table and some chairs."

"Does Dr. Cameron-Gordon work there late?"

"I don't know. He is always there when I leave in the evening."

"Does he never go outside the walls?"

"No."

"When he leaves the laboratory, what is to prevent him from walking out by one of the gates?"

"They are always locked, except when visitors come. Then a gate porter opens them. There is a small door in the wall used by the staff. It is opened for us when we arrive and again when we leave."

Moon Flower smiled. "That was the door, Shun-Hi, I watched until I saw you come out one evening. Do you remember?"

Shun-Hi turned her head and affectionately kissed the hand resting on her shoulder.

"Is Huan Tsung-Chao a good master?" Nayland Smith asked.

"Yes. He is kind to us all."

"But you would rather be with Dr. Cameron-Gordon again?"

"Oh, yes!"

"And the Master, do you have much to do with him when he is there?"

"No." Shun-Hi spoke shudderingly. "I should be afraid to go near him."

"Tell me, Shun-Hi," Sir Denis said, "is any watch kept in the gardens at night?"

"I don't know. I am never there at night. But I don't think so. It is just a summer house where his Excellency comes for a rest."

Nayland Smith nodded. "Do you take a tray to Dr. Cameron-Gordon every day?"

"Oh, no. Some days one of the other girls is sent."

"And does the same girl bring it back?"

"As a rule, yes. The doctor leaves it on the ledge. But the day I gave him the message, he waited until I came to return the tray and give me the reply."

Nayland Smith pulled at the lobe of his ear, thoughtfully. "So that if we gave you another message for Dr. Cameron-Gordon, it might be several days before you could deliver it?"

"Yes."

"Hm. That complicates matters."

Tony, who had listened to every word, broke in at this point. "It only means, Sir Denis, a few days more delay."

"Perhaps. But Fu-Manchu is merely a bird of passage in Szechuan. He may move on at any time. I have no idea in what way he's employing Cameron-Gordon's special knowledge. But as it's obviously of some value to Fu-Manchu, when one goes, the other goes with him."

Moon Flower's eyes opened widely. "Oh, I couldn't bear it. We are so near to him—and yet—"

"We have to face facts, Jeanie," Sir Denis said. "Even if we're given our chance, it may not come off. But I have a strong conviction that if we make no mistakes it will."

At a glass-topped table a man whose iron-gray hair, fresh complexion and closely trimmed gray moustache leant him something of the look of a Scottish sergeant-major, bent over a powerful microscope. He wore a white linen jacket, the scientist's field uniform. Whatever he was studying absorbed all his attention.

A faint sound made by an opening door failed to distract him.

The tall man who had entered, also in white, stood silent, watching.

Without removing his eye from the instrument, the student scribbled something on a pad which lay near his hand. He looked a while longer, then, standing up and completing the note he had made, sat down and turned to a globular lamp-glass, the top closed with cotton wool, standing in a Petri dish. Several sheets of damp filter paper lay in the bottom. He took up a lens and stared intently into the glass globe.

"I see, Doctor," came a sibilant voice from the shadowed doorway, "you are studying my new sandflies."

"Yes." The man addressed didn't even glance aside.

"Are you satisfied?"

"Yes. But you won't be."

"Why?"

"They are not absorbing the virus."

"It is fed to them."

"It is here, on the filter papers. But they reject it." He looked up for the first time. Light blue eyes blazed under shaggy eyebrows. "For your own filthy purpose, these new imports are useless."

Fu-Manchu walked slowly into the room, stood over the seated man, and smiled his icy smile.

"Your mulish obstinacy in ignoring my high purpose begins to annoy me." He spoke softly. "You are well aware of the fact that I do not strike at random. Only the guilty suffer. You persist in confusing my aims with those of the Communist fools who wrecked your mission hospital. You presume to classify my work with that of the ignorant, power-drunk demagogues who have forced their way into the Kremlin."

"Your methods are much the same."

There was a moment of tense silence, broken only by a rhythmic throbbing in the adjoining room. Fu-Manchu's clenched hands relaxed.

"You forget that I saved you from the mob who burned your home."

"By arresting me and making me a prisoner here. It was you who inspired the mob—for that purpose alone."

Fu-Manchu's voice was coldly calm when he spoke again. "Dr. Cameron-Gordon, I respect your knowledge. I respect your courage. But I cannot respect your blindness to the fact that our ideals are identical. My methods in achieving them are beyond your understanding. Be good enough to leave your work for an hour. I wish to talk to you."

"When I undertake a thing, though I may loathe it, I carry it out. My work here is not finished."

"You are dedicated to your studies, Doctor. That is why I admire you. Please come with me."

Dr. Cameron-Gordon shrugged his shoulders and stood up. He followed the tall figure to the room at the end of the long, low building which Fu-Manchu used as a rest room, sat down in a comfortable chair. Fu-Manchu opened a closet.

"May I offer you a Scotch and soda, Doctor?"

"Thank you, no." Cameron-Gordon sniffed. "But I have no objection to your smoking a pipe of opium. If you smoke enough the world will soon be rid of you."

Dr. Fu-Manchu smiled his mirthless smile. "If I told you for how many years I have used opium, you would not believe me. Opium will not rid the world of me."

He closed the closet and sat down on the couch.

"That's a pity," Cameron-Gordon commented dryly.

Fu-Manchu took a pinch of snuff, then pressed the tips of his fingers together. "I have tried many times, since you have been my guest—" Cameron-Gordon made a snorting sound—"to enlighten you concerning the aims of the Si-Fan. I have told you of the many distinguished men who work for the Order—"

"You mean who are slaves of the Order."

"I mean convinced and enthusiastic members. It is unavoidable, Doctor, if the present so-called civilization is not to perish, that some intellectual group, such as that which I mention, should put an end to the pretensions of the gang of impudent impostors who seek to create a Communist world. This done, the rest is easy. And the Si-Fan can do this."

"So you have told me. But your methods of doing it don't appeal to me. My experience with the Si-Fan isn't exactly encouraging."

Fu-Manchu continued calmly. "I have no desire to use coercion. Without difficulty, and by purely scientific means, I could exact your obedience."

"You mean you could drug me?"

"It would be simple. But it is a method which, in the case of a delicately adjusted brain such as yours, might impair your work. As I wish you to continue your researches during my absence, I have been thinking that your daughter—"

Cameron-Gordon came to his feet at a bound, fists clenched and fighting mad. In two strides he stood over Dr. Fu-Manchu.

"By God! speak another word of that threat and I'll strangle you with my bare hands!"

Fu-Manchu did not stir. He remained perfectly still, his lids half-towered over his strange eyes.

"I made no threat," he said softly. "I was thinking that your daughter would be left unprovided for if any rash behavior on your part should make her an orphan."

"In other words, unless I submit to you, I shall be liquidated."

"I did not say so. You can join the Si-Fan whenever you wish. You will enjoy complete freedom. You can practice any form of religion which may appeal to you. Your place of residence will be of your own choosing. Your daughter can live with you. All that I shall call upon you to do will be to carry out certain experiments. Their purpose will not concern you. My object is to crush Communism. You can help me to attain that goal."

Cameron-Gordon's clenched hands relaxed. Dr. Fu-Manchu's sophistry had not deceived him, but it had made him reflect.

"Thanks for the explanation," he said dourly. "I'll be thinking it over. Perhaps I can get back to my work, now?"

"By all means, Doctor." Fu-Manchu raised drooping lids and gave him a brief, piercing, green-eyed glance. "Return to your experiment."

CHAPTER SEVENTEEN

It was early next morning when Nayland Smith and Tony joined the stream of workers, many of them silk weavers, pouring through the narrow streets. Tony wore thick-rimmed glasses, a sufficient disguise. Shun-Hi hurried along ahead, and they kept her in sight.

On the outskirts of the town she was joined by two companions, evidently fellow servants. After, passing a large factory into which the crowd of workers was finally absorbed, they came to the country road leading to the summer villa of Huan Tsung-Chao. Sir Denis, Tony, and the three girls ahead of them were now all that remained of the former throng.

"Drop back a bit," Nayland Smith cautioned. "Those other girls might think we're following them from amorous motives." He grabbed Tony's arm. "In here!"

They stepped through an opening in a cactus hedge and found a path parallel to the road which bordered a large field of poppies.

"God!" Tony exclaimed. "What a crop!"

"The Reds have certainly stepped up the opium trade," Nayland Smith remarked.

They went ahead, guided by the girls' voices, and when these grew faint, they came out again onto the road. Shun-Hi and her friends had turned into a side path. Tony caught a glimpse of the three figures just before they were lost in the shadows of a cypress grove.

"We must chance it," Nayland Smith muttered. "Have to keep them in sight. I want a glimpse of this staff entrance Shun-Hi and Jeanie mentioned."

They had gone all of another mile before they saw the roof of a large house gleaming in the morning sun. It stood in the middle of what was evidently a considerable estate, and the narrow lane along which the girls were now hurrying was bordered by a high wall.

They had drawn up closer to the three.

"There's the entrance," Tony exclaimed suddenly. "They're just going in."

"So I see," Nayland Smith spoke quietly. "We must wait awhile, in case there are others to come. We might venture a little further and then take cover. That banyan twenty yards ahead will be good cover."

Three minutes later, having forced a way through tangled undergrowth, they stood in the shade of the huge tree. The gate in the wall was clearly in view. It was a metal-studded teak door, evidently of great strength. At the moment it remained open.

"Someone else is expected," Sir Denis muttered. They waited. And Tony, watching the open door in the wall, realized for the first time that the high wall alone separated two implacable enemies. The thought appalled him. He and Nayland Smith were alone; on the other side of the wall, in the person of the governor, all the strength of the Red regime was entrenched.

"Hullo! What's this?"

Nayland Smith grabbed his arm.

Four bearers appeared from somewhere along the lane, carrying the Chinese equivalent of a sedan chair. They stopped before the open door; set the chair down.

A tall man wearing a mandarin robe and a black cap with a coral bead came out and stepped into the chair. The bearers took it up and passed so close to the banyan that Sir Denis dragged Tony down onto his knees. The chair went by. Nayland Smith, still grasping his arm, stared into Tony's eyes.

"Dr. Fu-Manchu."

Neither spoke for a long minute. Then Tony said, "It's too optimistic to hope that he's leaving Szechuan."

"I'm afraid so," Nayland Smith agreed. "But, with a revolver in my pocket, I'm wondering if I should have missed such an opportunity."

Oddly enough, this aspect of the situation had never occurred to Tony. Only as Sir Denis spoke did he realize how deep an impression the personality of Fu-Manchu had made upon him. The regal dignity and consciousness of power which surrounded the Chinese doctor like a halo seemed to set him so far above common men.

"I wonder, too."

"Don't fall for the spell he casts, McKay. I admit he's a genius. But…"

Tony looked hard at Nayland Smith. "Could you do it?"

"Once I could have done it. Now that I have learned to assess the phenomenal brilliance of that great brain, I doubt myself. My hand would falter. But we can at least carry out our investigations without meeting Fu-Manchu. He, alone, would know me. You have no one to fear but the big Nubian."

They came out of their cover. The chair with its bearers had disappeared in the direction of the town. They walked to the door in the wall. Nayland Smith examined it carefully, turned away. "Pretty hopeless," he said.

The lane was deserted, and they followed the high wall for a quarter of a mile without finding another entrance. Nayland Smith scanned it yard by yard and at a point where the pink blossom of a peach tree evidently trained against the wall peeped over the top, he paused.

"Apparently an orchard. Do you think you could find the spot at night, McKay?"

"Quite sure."

"Good."

Tony asked no questions as they passed on. Another twenty yards and they came to a corner. The wall was continued at a right angle along an even narrower lane, a mere footpath choked with weeds. They forced a way through. Nayland Smith studied the wall with eager concentration. It ended where they had a prospect of a river, and turned right again on a wider road spanned by a graceful bridge from the grounds of the big house.

Tony saw a landing stage to which a motor cruiser was tied.

"That river will be the Tung Ho, I suppose," Nayland Smith muttered, staring up at the bridge, "and this will be the governor's watergate."

"He must be a wealthy man."

Sir Denis grinned. "Huan Tsung-Chao is a fabulously wealthy man. He's a survivor of imperial days, and God alone knows his age. How he came to hold his present position under the Peiping regime is a mystery."

"Why?"

"He is Dr. Fu-Manchu's chief of staff. I met him once and whatever else he may be, he is a gentleman, however misguided."

Tony then saw, several hundred yards up the road, what was

evidently a main entrance. A man in military uniform stood outside.

"What do we do now?" he asked.

"Turn back. I don't want that fellow to see us. Come on."

They retreated around the corner and made their way back along the wall.

Before a gate in a barbed-wire fence, Dr. Fu-Manchu stepped out of his chair. A soldier on duty there saluted the Master as he went in. There were flowering trees and shrubs in the enclosure surrounding a group of buildings of obviously recent construction. A path bordered by a cactus hedge led to the door of the largest of these.

The door was thrown open as Fu-Manchu appeared, and the Burmese doorman bowed low. Fu-Manchu ignored him and went on his way, walking slowly with his strange, catlike step. The place was unmistakably a hospital, with clean, white-walled corridors. Before a door at the end of one of these corridors, Fu-Manchu paused and pressed a button.

A trap masking a grille in the door slid aside and someone looked out. At almost the same moment, the door was opened. Matsukata, the Japanese physician, stood inside.

"Your report," Fu-Manchu demanded tersely.

"There is no change, Master."

"Show me the chart."

They went into a small dressing room. Fu-Manchu removed his robe and cap and put on a white jacket similar to the one worn by the Japanese. Matsukata turned away as Fu-Manchu completed his change of dress.

"Here is the chart, Master."

It was snatched from his hand. Dr. Fu-Manchu scanned it rapidly.

"You have checked everything—the temperature inside, the oxygen supply?"

"Everything."

Fu-Manchu walked out of the room and into a larger one equipped as an operating room. In addition to the operating table and other customary equipment, there were several quite unusual pieces here and one feature which would have arrested the attention of any modem surgeon.

This was a glass case, like those in which Egyptian mummies are exhibited, and the resemblance was heightened by the fact that it contained a lean, nude, motionless body. But here the resemblance ended.

The heavy case rested upon what were, apparently, finely adjusted scales. A dial with millesimal measurements recorded the weight of the case and its contents. A stethoscopic attachment to the body was wired to a kind of clock. There was an intake from a cylinder standing beside the case, a mechanism which showed the quality of the air inside, and two thermometers. An instrument for checking blood pressure was strapped to an arm of the inert gray figure and connected with a mercury manometer outside the case. There were also a number of electric wires in contact with the body.

Dr. Fu-Manchu checked everything with care, comparing what he saw with what appeared on the chart.

He began to pace the floor.

"Are you sure, Master," Matsukata ventured, "that in repairing the spinal fracture you did not injure the cord?"

Fu-Manchu halted as suddenly as if he had walked into a brick wall. Then he turned, and his eyes blazed murderously, madly.

"Are you presuming to question my surgery?" he shouted. "Am I, now, to return to Heidelberg, to the Sorbonne, to Edinburgh, and beg to be re-enrolled as a student—I who took highest honors at all of them?"

He was in the grip of one of those outbursts of maniacal frenzy which, years before, had led Nayland Smith and others to doubt his sanity.

Matsukata seemed to shrink physically. He became speechless.

Fu-Manchu raised clenched hands above his head. "God of China!" he cried, "give me strength to conquer myself or I shall kill this man!"

He dropped down onto a chair, sank his head in his hands. Matsukata began to steal away.

"Stand still!" Fu-Manchu commanded.

Matsukata stood still.

There was complete silence for several minutes. Then Dr. Fu-Manchu stood up. He was calm; the frenzy had passed.

"Prepare the cold room," he ordered. "I must re-examine the patient."

On his return from the early morning investigation, Nayland Smith's behavior was peculiar. After a hasty meal, he appeared dressed as a workingman. He grinned at Tony and Moon Flower.

"I'm off again," he announced. "All I want you two to do is to stay indoors until I come back. Can you bear it?"

Tony and Moon Flower exchanged glances. Tony's inclinations and his sense of duty were at war. "Can't I be of any use, Sir Denis?" he asked.

"There's not a thing you could do, McKay, that I can't do better alone." And off he went.

"Chi Foh." Moon Flower spoke almost in a whisper. "It's wonderful for us to be together again. I know that Sir Denis is working to rescue Father. But you must feel, as I do, that to stay inactive is dreadful."

Tony threw his arms around her. "You weren't inactive, Moon Flower, in finding Shun-Hi and I don't think it will be long before we are active again. I'm learning a lot about Sir Denis. When he tells me to stay put, I stay put. He's a grand man, and I'm glad to take his orders."

The interval of waiting, to these affianced lovers, was rapturous. But even with Moon Flower's arms around him, Tony had pangs of conscience. Nayland Smith was on the big job, and he was dallying.

As the day wore on and Sir Denis didn't return, this uneasiness became alarm.

Where had he gone? What was he doing?

With the coming of dusk, both were wildly uneasy. Tony's glimpse of Dr. Fu-Manchu that morning had sharpened his dread of the Master. He was painfully aware of the fact that if anything happened to Nayland Smith they would be helpless; two wanderers lost behind the second Bamboo Curtain.

Tony paced the room. Moon Flower rarely stirred from the window.

"If only I had some idea of where he went," Tony said desperately.

He heard a crisp step on the landing. Nayland Smith walked in.

"Thank God!" Tony said with relief.

Moon Flower turned in a flash. "I didn't see you on the street."

"No, Jeanie. I came another way and entered by the back door. I had an uneasy feeling I was being followed."

"I hope you were wrong," Tony said.

"So do I," Sir Denis admitted, opening the closet where they kept a scanty supply of liquor. "A stiff Scotch and soda is clearly indicated."

"I had hoped to hear from Shun-Hi," Moon Flower began.

"No luck today," Nayland Smith rapped. "I have seen her. She'll try again tomorrow. By that time we'll be ready to go into action."

Sir Denis grinned in his impish way. "I had to clear the course," he stated cryptically, and began to fill his pipe.

CHAPTER EIGHTEEN

Tony woke early on the following morning. Looking across the room which he shared with Nayland Smith, he saw that the bed was empty. He thought little about it, for Sir Denis's hours of rising were unpredictable. He took a shower, went into the living room, and lighted a cigarette.

When the woman who looked after their apartment came in to set the table for breakfast, he asked her, in Chinese, what time Sir Denis had gone out. They always spoke Chinese in the presence of the servants. She looked surprised and told him that it must have been before six o'clock, as no one had gone out since.

Moon Flower joined him half an hour later. "Isn't Sir Denis up yet?" she asked in surprise.

"Very much up," Tony told her. "He must have gone out around dawn."

She stared at him in a puzzled way. "He's behaving very oddly, isn't he? Of course, I know it all has something to do with getting Father free, but I wish he wouldn't scare us by these disappearances."

"Who's scaring you?" barked a voice from the direction of the doorway.

Tony turned—and there was Nayland Smith smiling at them. He wore his workman's clothes.

"Where on earth have you been?" Tony asked. "And at what time did you start?"

"I started some time before daylight, McKay. I've been finishing the job of clearing the course. All we're waiting for now is word from Cameron-Gordon."

During breakfast, in spite of Moon Flower's cross-examination, Nayland Smith evaded any explanation of his plans. "I believe, Jeanie, I have done all that can be done so far. Our next move will be touch-and-go. And I don't want to raise false hopes."

He spent the forenoon smoking his pipe near the window, constantly watching the passersby. Once he spoke aside to Tony, out of Moon Flower's hearing. "If they once suspected we were here, all my plans would be shattered."

Tony felt like a greyhound on the leash, and Moon Flower, reproachfully, retired to her own room.

During luncheon Nayland Smith tried to divert their gloomy thoughts with memories of his many encounters with Dr. Fu-Manchu, particularly those in which he had foiled the cunning Chinese scientist. "I'm only a moderately competent policeman. This man is a criminal genius. But I have had him on the mat more than once. Unfortunately, he always got up again."

The afternoon was passed in the same way; but when evening drew near, Nayland Smith's imperturbable calm began to show signs of breaking down. Several times he looked at his watch, then out the window again.

Suddenly he cried out, "Here she is!" and sprang to the door in his eagerness.

Shun-Hi, flushed and excited, came in. Moon Flower ran to meet her.

"Here it is, Miss Yueh Hua. The answer from your father."

Moon Flower almost snatched the folded sheet of paper right out of Shun-Hi's hand.

"Quick, Jeanie, is it for tonight?" Nayland Smith snapped.

She read, quickly, tears in her eyes, then looked up. "Yes. Tonight."

In the dusk, Tony and Nayland Smith set out. They had weathered a bad storm with Moon Flower.

"I simply dare not take her, McKay," Sir Denis said. "I understand her eagerness to see her father, but if anything goes wrong tonight, we shall have walked into hell. Whatever happens to you and me, Jeanie will be safe, if she does what I told her to do. You heard my instructions to Lao Tse-Mung. If we get Cameron-Gordon clear, the plans are laid for Jeanie and her father to fly to Hong Kong. Your capture of the Chinese manuscript was a divine miracle. We may have Dr. Fu-Manchu at our mercy. But Skobolov's correspondence has given me ideas about the Soviet research centre. We are going to take a look at the centre, McKay."

They followed the route which they took before, when Shun-Hi had led them to the staff entrance of General Huan's house. But tonight the streets were not thronged. In one quarter, a fringe of which touched their route, they could see lighted lanterns in adjoining streets, and hear barbaric music, but it was soon left behind.

Once clear of the outskirts of the town, two workingmen and their moon-shadows walked along the highway.

There was something melancholy in the empty countryside, in the breathless stillness, which bred in Tony's mind a sense of foreboding. Nayland Smith had been silent for some time. Suddenly he spoke.

"Your automatic is ready, I take it, McKay?"

And the words suggested to Tony that Sir Denis was feeling the same apprehension.

"Yes, sure."

"So's my revolver. Always want to be prepared."

Tony was obsessed by an urgent need to talk, and so, "You said you had cleared the course," he said, trying to speak lightly. "To which part of the course did you refer?"

"The last hundred yards," Nayland Smith replied, and fell silent again.

Twenty paces on, he stopped suddenly and grasped Tony's arm. "Listen."

Tony stood completely still and strained his ears. He could hear nothing.

"What do you think you heard?" he asked Nayland Smith in a hushed voice.

"Someone behind us. But there's no one in sight."

But, as they resumed their march, Tony knew that the shadow which had fallen upon his spirits had also touched Nayland Smith.

They reached the point where, before, they had turned into the poppy field, but now kept to the high road. Soon they were on the path which Shun-Hi and her friends had followed and deep in the shadow of the cypresses. Tony's spirits sank even lower in the darkness.

Nayland Smith pulled up, stopped him with a touch.

A weird, plaintive wail rose in the night, and then died away.

"Stupid of me," Sir Denis murmured. "For one unpleasant moment I thought it was a dacoit. Just a night hawk."

They came to the lane bordering the high wall. Nayland Smith looked swiftly to right and left before stepping out. The side on which they stood, opposite the wall, lay in shadow. "All clear. Come on!"

Almost silent in their straw sandals, they moved on, nearer to the door in the wall. In the shade of the banyan, Nayland Smith turned aside, plunging into undergrowth. Tony followed. He was completely at a loss until Sir Denis produced a flashlight and shone it on the tangled roots of the great tree.

"Look!"

Tony looked and was astounded by what he saw.

A long, slender bamboo ladder lay there.

"Always glad to learn from the enemy, McKay. This clears the course from here to the laboratory where Cameron-Gordon is waiting for us."

"You still have me guessing."

Nayland Smith laughed. "This ladder is light enough for a child to carry and it's long enough to reach the top of General Huan's wall. It's also strong enough to support a man of reasonable weight."

"But where did you get it?"

"I found a friendly carpenter. Told him I was a gardener employed in a place where there were tall trees to be pruned. He had the ladder ready by evening. I collected it and carried it here early in the morning before anyone was about."

He dragged the ladder from the roots of the tree.

They returned to the lane, Tony carrying the ladder on his shoulder. "I have to look out for the pear tree?"

"Right. Go ahead. I want to keep an eye on the lane behind."

Tony tramped on. Promise of action blew aside the cloud of foreboding which had crept over him. And soon, against the bright sky, he saw pear blossoms peeping over the wall like a scene in a Japanese water-color painting.

"All clear," Nayland Smith called. "Set the ladder up, McKay."

Tony found a spot among the weeds at the foot of the wall where he could make the base of the ladder firm, and gingerly maneuvered its delicate frame into place.

"All ready."

"Stand by, McKay. I must make sure that the trellis is strong enough to be safe. We may want to leave in a hurry."

Nayland Smith went up the ladder with an agility surprising in a man no longer young. Tony watched, breathless with excitement. Sir Denis climbed over the wall and began to climb down on the other side. When his head was level with the pink blossoms, he spoke again.

"Follow on," he instructed. "Safe as an oak staircase."

"Do I leave the ladder?"

"No choice, McKay. If it's moved, we'll have to drop from the wall."

Tony was up in a matter of seconds and looked over the top. He saw a well-planted orchard: pear trees, plums, and other fruits. Nayland Smith stood below.

Tony swung his leg over, found a stout branch, and scrambled down.

"What's our direction, Sir Denis?"

"Not quite sure. Must get my bearings."

Nayland Smith stood there in the shadow of the wall, tugging at his ear.

"Shun-Hi tried to explain the location of the laboratory."

"She did. And it's clear in my mind, now. Follow on."

They had to make a wide detour around the house. The property was landscaped as a pleasure garden, with lily ponds and streams of running water and with miniature waterfalls amid a blaze of rockery flowers. In the moonlight it was entrancing.

The laboratory, when at last they sighted it, proved to be partly screened in a grove of orange trees. This was all to the good. It was an ugly building, evidently of recent construction; a long, narrow hut, but much larger than Tony had thought it would be.

"We have to show ourselves in the moonlight to reach the orange trees, which troubles me," Nayland Smith said. "But at this point we're not in view from the house."

"There isn't a light on in the house," Tony pointed out.

"That's what bothers me. Let's make a dash for it." They raced across the bright patch of moonlight and into the shadow of the trees.

Two windows of the laboratory building were lighted—a small one near the door and a larger one at the side of the hut. Tony pushed forward, but Nayland Smith stood still, looking back, listening. He said nothing, but joined Tony on a narrow path which led to the door.

He rapped on the panels. The light in the window disappeared. The door opened, and a man in a white coat peered out.

"Smith. Quickly, come in! Who's with you?"

"Tony McKay, one of us."

They entered in darkness. The door was closed again and a light sprang up.

Tony saw a tiny room with a table and two chairs, just as Shun-Hi had described. The man in the white coat spoke hoarsely.

"Thank God you found me, Smith, I didn't know you were in China. And God bless Jeanie for getting my message through. I didn't want to show a light when I opened the door. I never know when I'm being watched."

"Nor do I," Nayland Smith said. "I suggest we start."

Cameron-Gordon had his hand in a fervent gesture of greeting. "Wait just a few moments, Smith. I want you to see the kind of work I do." He transferred the handshake to Tony. "You must be quite a man to be here, and I'm glad to meet you."

He opened a door, beckoned them to follow. They did so reluctantly.

On the threshold they halted simultaneously. There was a muffled buzzing sound and a strange, repulsive odor. The place was lined by glass cases, in which, as Cameron-Gordon switched on the light, they saw feverish activity going on. The cases were filled with insects, some with wings and some without; huge flies, bloated spiders, ants, centipedes, scorpions.

"My God!" Tony muttered.

"I have seen something like this before," Nayland Smith said, "in another of Fu-Manchu's establishments."

"My dear Smith"—Cameron-Gordon was alight with the enthusiasm of the specialist—"he is doing work here which, if it were used for the good of humanity, would make his name immortal. His knowledge of entomology is stupendous."

"I have had some experience with it," Nayland Smith rapped dryly. "'My little allies,' he once called these horrors."

Cameron-Gordon ignored the interruption. "His experiments, Smith, are daring beyond what is allowed to be known by God-fearing men. He has bred hybrids of the insect world which never before existed except for sufferers of delirium tremens. I'll show you some. But he has also prepared drugs from these sources which, if made available to physicians, would almost certainly wipe out the ravages of many fatal diseases."

"Tell me, Doctor," Tony said faintly, "what is *that?*" He was staring at a case which contained an enormous centipede of a dull red color. It was fully a foot long and was moving around its glass prison with horrible, febrile activity.

"A Mexican specimen of the *morsitans* species. Twice its hitherto-known largest size. From its toxin he hopes to prepare an inoculation giving immunity from cholera. One of my duties is to extract the toxin."

"And what about this hideous spider?"

"Known in New Zealand as a katipo, but in this instance, crossed with a tarantula. Its sting is deadly. Dr. Fu-Manchu has made a poison from that creature's toxin which when swallowed, and it's tasteless, kills in five minutes; injected, kills instantly. Look at that colony of red ants. Another hybrid species. They multiply from hundreds to millions in a short time. They eat anything. Set loose here in China, they would turn Asia into a desert from the sea to the Himalayas in a few months."

Nayland Smith was glancing anxiously at his watch. But Cameron-Gordon remained in the grip of his enthusiasm.

"These," he pointed, "are plague fleas. They are reinforced with plague cultures. One bite would mean the end. I have to feed them."

Sir Denis broke in. "These cases filled with buzzing flies particularly interest me. What are they?"

"Tsetse flies," Cameron-Gordon told him, turning. "Each one of the cases is kept at a different temperature, which I regulate. The first, which you're looking at, is kept at tropical heat, the normal temperature for these insects. The second is sub-tropical. The third is temperate. And the fourth is arctic. So far, we have failed with the fourth. But some of the flies in there are still alive."

"So I see."

"They are fed on blood plasma, charged with the trypanosoma of sleeping sickness. They are so reinforced that their bite induces a form of a disease which goes through its entire stages in a matter of days, instead of months. They could operate anywhere short of the Arctic Circle. They are utterly damnable!"

Nayland Smith looked grimly at Tony. "Now we know how Skobolov died."

And, as he spoke, the light went out.

"I fear," a cold, sibilant voice said, "that you know too much, Sir Denis."

In complete darkness, Tony, his heart beating a tattoo, realized that he stood closest to the door. He reached it, and found it unopenable.

"We're trapped, McKay!" Nayland Smith said. "What about—"

"What about the other door, you were thinking, Sir Denis?" came the mocking voice. "Unfortunately, as it belongs to my laboratory, I make a point of keeping it locked."

Tony, cool again after that first shock, began to peer through the darkness in the direction from which the voice came. His hand closed over the butt of his automatic. He had seen something.

High up at the end of this home of insect horrors, he saw a square patch of dim light. He raised his automatic and fired.

The odor of the discharge mingled with the other unpleasant smell which haunted the place. Vibration caused a rattle of glass, but it came from the surrounding cases. Then the silence was complete again, except for the faint buzzing of the tsetse flies and whispering sounds made by some of the other inhabitants of the cases.

"No good, McKay," Nayland Smith said sharply. "I saw that opening, too."

"It's over the door of my workroom," Cameron-Gordon whispered. "That's where he is."

His words were answered by a harsh laugh from Dr. Fu-Manchu.

"Since the arrival of my old acquaintance, Sir Denis, in China, I have made it a practice to look in, unobtrusively, whenever you have remained late at work, Dr. Cameron-Gordon. Tonight I seem to have disturbed your showing your friends this small collection of rare specimens."

"Enough of this idle chatter," Nayland Smith barked angrily. "You have trapped us. Very well, come and take us!"

"Sir Denis, how strangely you misread my purpose. If I desired your death, it would be necessary only to shatter any one of the cases of specimens surrounding you—which I assure you I could do without exposing myself to your fire. Should you prefer the tsetse flies? That would be a lingering death. Or perhaps the fleas and the painful result of bubonic plague?"

"You're not a man, you're a demon!" Tony rasped.

"I have knowledge which few men possess, Mr. McKay, that is your name, I believe. And as you are clearly a man of courage, possibly you would prefer to try to repel in the dark the attack of my *katipo,* tarantula? He is a strangely active nocturnal creature."

"Stop talking!" Nayland Smith shouted. "Words don't frighten us. Smash everything in the place, if you like."

"That is indeed the familiar spirit of the British policeman. But, for your very stubbornness I admire you, Sir Denis. Dr. Cameron-Gordon is useful to me, and I believe I could use the qualities of Mr. McKay also."

"You never will," Tony assured him.

"Let me explain myself," the cold, emotionless voice continued. "There are more ways than by drugs, or physical pain, to enforce obedience. One of these means I hold in my hands. There is no place for heroics. Dismiss any plans you may have made. I assure you that you have no alternative other than acceptance of my terms—whatever they may be."

CHAPTER NINETEEN

Tony opened his eyes; looked around. He closed his eyes again. This was part of the dream. In the part which had passed earlier he had wandered in a strange paradise. There were trees laden with blossoms he had never seen before and the ground upon which he trod was carpeted with flowers. The air was filled with their intoxicating perfume.

He rested under one of the trees, from which a gentle breeze dropped fragrant petals from time to time. A gracefully beautiful girl had joined him, seated herself beside him. She carried a flask of wine and two crystal glasses. She smiled, and her dark eyes challenged him provocatively. She filled the glasses.

"You will drink with me?" she whispered, handing him a glass. "I belong to you, and so let us drink together."

Tony hesitated. She wore a gauzy robe and through its mist every line of her shapely body was visible. She placed her arms around his neck. Her ripe lips were very near. Some swift revulsion swept over him. He dashed his glass to the ground, and sudden darkness fell…

When the dark cloud passed, he found himself in another part of the garden. A sweet voice, a woman's voice, spoke from the shadow of a flowering bush near where Tony lay.

"Why are you so sad?" the voice asked. "You are young and the world is before you. There is nothing to prevent you from rising to the greatest heights. May I talk to you?"

"Yes," he remembered saying.

He was joined by a fair woman as beautiful as the dark siren who had offered him wine. She seated herself beside him on the mossy bank. She had strange violet eyes, alight with intelligence.

"Together," she said softly, "we could go so very far."

Tony looked into the violet eyes, and as he looked they seemed to turn green, the fair features became yellowish and he found himself staring into the saturnine face of Dr. Fu-Manchu.

So the dream had ended, and now, he thought, it was continuing.

He opened his eyes again.

The wonderful garden had gone and with it the beautiful women and the hypnotic face of Fu-Manchu. He lay, not among flowers, but on a cushioned divan. Looking around, he still saw what he had seen before: a small room luxuriously furnished in the Oriental manner. The only light came from a shaded lantern hung from the ceiling. But there were rich rugs on the floor, lacquered objects gleamed from the shadows. There was a faint odor of sandalwood.

He sat up, conscious of a swimming feeling, but with no trace of headache to explain what he supposed to have been delirium. He tried to stand up. He couldn't. Looking down, angrily, at his ankles, he saw that they were secured by a tiny cord of something that resembled catgut. He put his heels together and tried to snap it.

The effort was useless. The fastenings pierced his skin, and he knew that any further attempts would only cut the tendons.

And, in that moment of acute pain, real memory came, bridging the mirage which had clouded his mind. He remembered that last scene in the insect vivarium lined with cases of loathsome creatures, remembered the mocking words of Fu-Manchu.

Then had come that perfumed cloud, oblivion...

A heavy curtain was silently drawn aside, and Dr. Fu-Manchu came in.

He wore a yellow robe. A sort of satanic majesty seemed to radiate from the tall figure. Silent, he stood watching Tony. Then, at last, he spoke.

"Your impersonation of Chi Foh, the fisherman, was excellent. You almost deceived me. I congratulate you."

Tony said nothing.

"The gas which overcame you is a preparation perfected by me some years ago. If any of it had penetrated the cases, it would not have affected the creatures confined there."

It was hard to sit and listen to that cold voice. Dr. Fu-Manchu spoke English with careful perfection and his manner was that of a professor addressing a class of students.

"What a pity," Tony commented.

"I note that you are imitating the brand of repartee favored by Sir Denis Nayland Smith. It is usually prompted by bravado in moments of danger. I am completely acquainted with the psychological features of Sir Denis's character. I endeavored to learn something of your own, particularly of one aspect, during the time that you remained under the influence of the drug. Its composition renders the subject peculiarly impressionable to what is sometimes termed hypnotic suggestion."

Tony was listening intently now.

"I projected onto your brain the images of two desirable women who are members of my organization. There was no trace of sexual

172

reaction. You rejected their overtures. In fact you dispelled the second image, for I saw recognition of myself dawning in your eyes. But I had learned what I wanted to know. You are completely devoted to one woman. And I think I know her name."

Tony found himself alone again. Dr. Fu-Manchu had stepped silently to the draped opening, raised the curtain, and silently disappeared.

He could detect no sound of any kind. Where was he? What place was this? And where were Nayland Smith and Cameron-Gordon? He stood up and learned that by taking short, mincing steps he could walk.

First, he crossed to the curtain from behind which Fu-Manchu had entered and retired. He raised the heavy brocade. He saw a blank wall. That it masked a door was perfectly obvious, but to find out how to open it was another matter.

He hobbled around the room, examining the wall foot by foot.

The room had no window and no door.

For one horrifying moment panic touched him with its icy finger.

Except that it was exotically furnished, this place was no better than an oubliette, one of those dreadful medieval dungeons, without any exit other than an inaccessible trap. He had seen one in an ancient French castle.

He returned to the settee and tried to recover composure, get himself in hand.

That he might be left in this luxurious cell to starve to death was a nightmare he could safely dismiss. Dr. Fu-Manchu had other plans for him; he had spoken of terms which, "whatever they might be," he must accept.

He wanted to shout out curses on Fu-Manchu, that cold-blooded monster who used human emotions as ingredients in a scientific formula. But he smothered the useless words, clutched his head and groaned.

How long a time had elapsed since that moment when, surrounded by obscene insects, they had heard the sardonic voice of Dr. Fu-Manchu? He could have been unconscious for hours, days, weeks! The devilish genius who had them all in his power possessed medical knowledge which, as Cameron-Gordon had said, properly belonged to the future of science.

Tony groped in his Chinese garments. He was desperately thirsty, and a smoke might steady his nerves. His automatic was gone, but a packet of cigarettes and a lighter remained. He lighted a cigarette.

As he blew smoke from his lips he noted that it hung motionless in the stagnant air. There was little or no ventilation.

Sitting there, watching the smoke, trying to conquer useless anger and to think constructively, he became aware of two curious facts. The first, smoke clouds began to swirl; second, the air grew suddenly cold.

A premonition swept into his mind. He dropped the cigarette in a jade bowl which lay on a table near the divan, and stood up.

The curtain masking the hidden opening was moving. It was swept aside.

The gaunt figure of a man wearing only a loincloth stood there, looking into the room.

His neck was fixed in a brace which seemed to make his head immovable, for he never turned it in the slightest degree. The ghastly gray features and fishlike eyes in the rigid head were indescribably revolting. There was a long scar over the creature's heart.

But, crowning terror, this apparition unmistakably was that of the Cold Man whom he had killed, whose body, with a broken neck, he had seen lying at the foot of a tree near the wall of Lao Tse-Mung's house!

Tony stifled a cry of horror. He became cold as though his spine had frozen, incapable of action.

The gray thing spoke. Its voice resembled something on a worn-out record.

"Follow."

Very slowly, the gray figure turned, never moving the rigid neck. A black opening in the wall gaped behind him. The temperature of the room had become perceptibly lower. Tony, fists clenched convulsively, hesitated. Every human instinct prompted him to refuse to follow a thing which he could only believe to be of another world.

He overcame that helpless inertia which had seized him and took a deep breath. Dead or alive, the creature which had said "Follow" offered a way out of the prison in which he was trapped. But perhaps this was another dream, a further example of Dr. Fu-Manchu's psychological examinations—a test of his courage.

Tony followed. Slowly, because of the fastenings around his ankles; fearfully, because he was uncertain if he dreamt or was awake.

Ahead, silhouetted against a lighted opening, he could see the mummylike figure moving. He kept his distance. Even the narrow passage was chilled by the creature's presence. There was a short stair. He allowed the gray thing to reach the top before he followed, and found himself in a white-walled corridor, with doors opening to right and left. The corridor was empty.

Before one of these doors, the gray figure paused, pressed a bell and went on, moving mechanically like an automaton. When Tony came to the door—a sliding door—he found it wide open. He hesitated, glanced along the lighted passage. His phantom guide had disappeared.

He looked into a small room. The only illumination came from one wall of the room which appeared to be made of glass.

Three chairs were set facing the glass wall, and two of them were occupied.

"Hullo, McKay." Nayland Smith's unmistakably snappy speech. "You're rather late. But the curtain hasn't gone up yet."

As Tony stepped in, the sliding door closed noiselessly behind him.

He made his way to the vacant chair next to Nayland Smith and sat down. Dr. Cameron-Gordon, his head in his hands, occupied the third chair. Somewhere below, Tony could see through the glass wall, a large, dimly lighted place masked in vague shadows. Sir Denis grasped his hand.

"Keep smiling, McKay. I don't know what all this is about any more than you do. But we're still alive."

Then Cameron-Gordon's voice. "It's all over, Smith. What will become of Jeanie when we disappear for good?"

"Don't worry," Nayland Smith said. "We're in a tight corner, but at least we're all together."

Cameron-Gordon sighed and dropped his head into his hands again.

"I was led here by the dacoit we buried in the cypress grove," Tony whispered to Sir Denis. "It is supernatural!"

"Nothing is supernatural where Dr. Fu-Manchu is concerned. You may recall that the dacoit was dug up again!"

"What about it?"

"I have known of others buried as dead who have been disinterred by Fu-Manchu and restored to life."

"But a man with a broken neck?"

"Clever surgeons have mended broken necks before now. And

176

Dr. Fu-Manchu is probably the greatest surgeon the world has ever known."

As Nayland Smith stopped speaking, Tony noted for the first time how completely silent the cabinet in which they were assembled seemed to be! Not a sound was audible from outside its walls... until suddenly the stillness was broken by a voice, apparently the voice of someone in the room. But no one else was in the room.

"I am instructed," the modulated voice said, "to explain the purpose of what you are about to see. This is a soundproof observation room which both I and the Master use frequently. He is about to pay his daily visit to the *necropolites,* known locally as Cold Men—a duty which falls on me when the Master is absent."

"Dr. Matsukata," Cameron-Gordon muttered, "Fu-Manchu's chief technical assistant."

"Is that so?" Nayland Smith asked. "Why don't you join us, Dr. Matsukata, instead of speaking on radio?"

"I am following my instructions. Be so good, Sir Denis, as to listen to what I am here to tell you."

"Seems we have no choice," Tony commented.

The precise voice continued. "I believe you have already made the acquaintance of a *necropolite* and must have noted the unusual qualities which these creatures possess. In certain respects they resemble the Haitian zombies, whose existence has been disputed in some quarters. In fact, in certain respects, the process of reanimation is similar, but superior. They work as automata, being entirely controlled by the power miscalled hypnotic suggestion. Other than by complete disintegration, their faculties are indestructible. Thus, the *necropolite* is perfectly equipped to carry out dangerous missions."

"You're telling me nothing," Tony broke in. "But there's one thing you might tell me: What is a Japanese doing in Fu-Manchu's gang?"

"For a friend of Sir Denis Nayland Smith, you betray remarkable ignorance of the Order of the Si-Fan," Matsukata answered heatedly. "Its membership is not confined to China. It includes the whole of Asia, the Near East, many parts of Europe, and America. Its secret power is at least equal to that of Communism."

Light sprang up in the dim place below, and Tony found himself looking down into a morgue.

Nearly a score of gray bodies lay there in two rows, one row on the right and one on the left. But here the resemblance to a morgue ended. They lay, not on stone slabs, but on neat hospital cots.

"The *necropolites*," said Matsukata. "This clinic was constructed for the purpose of creating and maintaining them. They represent the Master's supreme achievement, for they are dead men who live again at his command. The process of reducing their bodies to the low temperature, at which, alone, reanimation can be brought about is too technical for description here. But I should be glad to discuss it, later, with Dr. Cameron-Gordon."

"Thank you, no," Cameron-Gordon muttered. "I want to keep what little sanity I have left."

"Be good enough to watch closely what takes place now. I must explain that a *necropolite* retains in his living-death state, whatever useful qualities were his in normal life, as well as his physical appetites or vices. Without occasional gratification of the latter, the creature's usefulness deteriorates. Watch carefully."

Tony was watching more than carefully. He was trying hard to convince himself that this thing was reality, that he wasn't lost again in a nightmare. Nayland Smith's crisp voice came to reassure him.

"I warned you, McKay, that if we made a mistake, we should walk into hell."

Dr. Fu-Manchu came into the ward below with its rows of gray corpses. He wore a white coat, and his manner showed the cool detachment that marks the specialist visiting a hospital ward. A white-coated orderly followed, pushing a glass-topped cabinet on rubber wheels. He was sallow-faced, but looked European.

Not a sound penetrated to the observation room, and Matsukata remained silent.

Dr. Fu-Manchu stopped beside the first cadaver at the end of the row and made a swift, skillful examination. He spoke over his shoulder to the orderly. The man charged a hypodermic syringe; handed it to him. Fu-Manchu gave an injection, not in the arm, but in the breast of the still body, and passed on to the next.

This singular proceeding continued until every cot had been visited. Two of the Cold Men received no injection.

As Fu-Manchu walked out with his strange, feline step, followed by the orderly wheeling the glass cabinet, three or four of the Cold Men first treated began to stir.

Tony found himself shivering.

"My God, it's insane!" Cameron-Gordon whispered.

Matsukata spoke again. "The Master has detected symptoms in two of the *necropolites* which necessitated their removal to surgery for further examination."

Almost as he ceased speaking, two stretchers were carried in and the two Cold Men placed on them and carried out.

"The most instructive feature of the treatment," the smooth Japanese voice went on, "will now begin. The Master will project to each creature the images appropriate to its particular appetite when it was a normal man. To one, the figure of its enemy; to another, a banquet of its favorite food; to a third, the image of a seductive woman—and so forth."

Now the Cold Men were rising up, moving gray arms

convulsively. All seemed to be crying out.

"They are calling for *Looma*," Matsukata explained. "By this name they know a drink which transports them to a dream life where there is no satiety. One can kill his enemy a hundred times, another eat and drink without experiencing repletion, a third enjoy the pleasures of love indefinitely. Something like the promised paradise of Mohammed."

"Don't they murder one another?" Tony asked shakily.

"They cannot leave their cots. Their movements are restricted by a length of slender cord, such as that which is attached to your ankles. They are about to receive their instructions."

Dr. Fu-Manchu returned, alone. He carried a lamp of unusual design. The light of this lamp was shone into the face of the Cold Man until his twitching and mouthing ceased. Then, Fu-Manchu rested his long fingers on the creature's temples and stared into its eyes. This routine was continued until all had been dealt with.

"Now comes *Looma*, their wine of paradise," Matsukata said softly.

As Dr. Fu-Manchu went out, a nurse in a trim white uniform came in, followed by the same orderly pushing the glass cabinet. It now carried a large glass jug filled with some liquid of a color resembling chartreuse, and some small glasses. The orderly filled the glasses and the nurse carried each to a Cold Man. In every case it was grasped avidly and swallowed in one eager draft.

But Tony scarcely followed what took place after the appearance of the nurse.

For the nurse was *Moon Flower.*

CHAPTER TWENTY

Tony's impressions of the next few minutes were chaotic. The frantic behavior of Cameron-Gordon, the crisp, soothing words of Nayland Smith, the tumult in his own mind, built up a jungle of frustrated hopes, terror, and abject misery in which the details of what actually occurred were lost.

He knew that the tiny tough shackles which confined their ankles had been dexterously and swiftly removed by a smiling Chinese mechanic. The man used an instrument resembling a small electric buzz saw.

And now the three of them were assembled in a room which reminded him of that in which he had been confined, except that it was larger. There was a low, round table in the center, and on it lay a note in small, legible characters which Nayland Smith picked up and read aloud.

"You may refresh yourselves as you please. I beg you to do so. Chinese hospitality forbids me to poison my guests. Sir Denis will assure you that my word is inviolable, Fu-Manchu."

Nayland Smith had just finished reading the letter when the door opened and two Chinese servants came in carrying full trays. They placed on the table a delicate meal of assorted dishes, a variety of wines, a bottle of Napoleon brandy, Scotch whiskey, a number of glasses and an English siphon of soda water. One of the servants uncorked all the bottles, placing the white wines in ice, and withdrew.

Nayland Smith grinned almost happily. "Let's make the best of it, and prepare for the worst."

"We'll all be drugged," Cameron-Gordon said.

Sir Denis held up the note. "This is the first example of Fu-Manchu's handwriting I have seen," he declared. "But it must obviously be genuine. I accept his word for I have never known him to break it."

Cameron-Gordon groaned. "Right or wrong, a shot of brandy is what I need."

"It would do none of us any harm," Sir Denis agreed, and poured out three liberal tots. "A compromise is going to be offered. It will be one we can't accept. But let us all sharpen our wits, and have something to eat."

But Cameron-Gordon made a very poor attempt. "How did that cunning fiend get his hands on Jeanie?" he asked in a voice of despair.

"I suspect," Sir Denis told him, "because of her own obstinacy."

"Meaning what?" Tony wanted to know.

"Meaning that I detected, or thought that I detected, the footsteps of someone following us. Jeanie is high spirited, and as nearly fearless as any woman I ever met. My guess is that Jeanie was the follower. We have even to suppose that she climbed the bamboo ladder and was actually in the garden when Fu-Manchu saw her."

"God help her," Cameron-Gordon groaned, "no one else can, now."

"I don't agree," Nayland Smith rapped in his sudden fashion. "There are weak spots in Fu-Manchu's armor. I think I can find one. But leave the talking to me."

Presently the Chinese servants reappeared, cleared the table, leaving only the brandy, and served coffee. They also brought cigars and cigarettes, port and a number of liqueurs.

"It's evidently dinner time," Sir Denis remarked when they went out. "I had an idea it might be luncheon."

"I have lost all track of time," Tony confessed. "My wrist watch is missing."

"All our watches are missing. We're not intended to know the time."

They had finished their coffee, and Cameron-Gordon sat deep in silent gloom, when the door opened again.

The huge Nubian stepped in. He wore some kind of uniform, had a revolver in a holster and a tarboosh on his head.

"March out." He had a deep, negroid voice. "One at a time. I will follow."

Nayland Smith glanced wryly at Tony, shrugged his shoulders. "You go first, McKay, then Cameron-Gordon. I'll bring up the rear."

The big man stood stiffly beside the open door, his hand on the butt of his revolver, as they filed out. Tony was seized by sudden misgivings. To what ordeal were they being taken? He dared not allow himself to think of Moon Flower.

At the end of a short passage he came to a flight of stairs.

"Go down," the deep voice ordered.

Tony went down. He was in one of the white-walled corridors which he had seen before. His fellow captives followed silently. He came to a cross-passage.

"Right turn."

He obeyed. He was a cadet again, being ordered about by a drill-sergeant.

The cross-passage ended in what appeared to be a vestibule. It was well lighted. He could see a large double door which might be the main entrance to the building.

"Halt."

The tone of command was unmistakable. This big African was an ex-soldier.

Tony halted, standing stiffly upright, then recovered himself, turned, and looked back. Cameron-Gordon was grim and angry, but Nayland Smith grinned reassuringly. The Nubian pointed to a long wooden bench.

"Sit down."

They sat down. Tony was assessing their chances of overpowering the man by a simultaneous attack. But even assuming that the double doors opened on freedom, how far could they go, and how would it help Moon Flower?

Nayland Smith seemed to read his thoughts, for he caught his eye and shook his head as a side door opened and two stocky Burmese came out.

Tony submitted to having his eyes scientifically bandaged. He imagined, rather than knew, that his companions were undergoing the same indignity. Next he was raised to his feet and led out into the open air. He was helped into a vehicle. A slight odor of petrol told him that it was an automobile. He guessed it was a limousine.

All three were packed into the back seat, the door was closed, and the car started. The engine had the velvet action of a Rolls.

"No talking," came the deep African voice.

The big Nubian was still with them.

A dreadful idea crossed Tony's mind. They were being taken to the jail at Chia-Ting! The thought seemed to chill his blood. Once inside that grim prison they would be lost to the world. Even Sir Denis, with all the power of Great Britain behind him, would merely be listed as missing.

But the horror was quickly dismissed. The car stopped long before they could have reached Chia-Ting, and he was hauled out. Unseen hands guided him through what he knew was a garden by the faint fragrance of flowers.

He was led onto a softly carpeted floor and piloted upstairs. He could hear the stumbling footsteps of his friends who followed. He was thrust down in a chair. And at last, the bandage was removed from his eyes.

Tony blinked, for a light shone directly on his face. For a while, he couldn't get accustomed to the glare after the complete darkness. But at last he did.

He saw a luxuriously furnished room. There were rich Chinese rugs, cabinets in which rare porcelain vases gleamed, trophies of arms, openings veiled by silk curtains. The lighting was peculiar. It came from a shaded lamp, the shade so constructed that light shone fully on his face and on the faces of his two companions. This lamp stood on a long lacquered desk, its gleaming surface littered with a variety of objects: books, manuscripts, some curious antique figures on pedestals, a small gong, and several queer-looking objects which were completely strange to him.

But these things he saw clearly later. His first impression of them was a vague one. For his attention became focused upon the man who sat behind the lacquered desk, wearing a plain yellow robe, his long-fingered hands resting on the desk before him. Owing to the cunning construction of the lampshade, his face was half shadowed.

With green eyes glinting under partly lowered lids, Dr. Fu-Manchu sat passively regarding the three trapped men.

"It is a long time, Sir Denis," he said softly, "since I had the privilege of entertaining you. I trust you enjoyed your supper?"

"Oh, it was supper? It was excellent."

"Prepared by a first-class French chef."

"Tell him if he cares to come to London, I can find him better employment."

Dr. Fu-Manchu took a pinch of snuff. "Incorrigible as always. In our many years' association I cannot recall that you ever admitted defeat."

Nayland Smith didn't reply. The green eyes were turned upon Tony, and he felt, again, the horrible sensation that they looked not at him, but clear through him.

"You have proved yourself a nuisance, Captain McKay," the sibilant voice continued, "but not a serious menace. Suppose I offered you your freedom, on two conditions?"

"What conditions?"

"One, that you married Miss Cameron-Gordon."

Tony's throat grew dry. "And the other?"

"That you both took the oath of allegiance to the Order of the Si-Fan."

Tony turned, met a look from the haggard eyes of Cameron-Gordon who cried out, "I don't understand. I didn't know you were even acquainted."

"We were thrown together for a long time, sir. I love your daughter deeply, sincerely. And she has consented to marry me, with your approval... but not until you are free."

"I have already offered Dr. Cameron-Gordon his freedom," Fu-Manchu murmured.

"On the same terms," Cameron-Gordon began, then stopped, sank his head in his hands.

Nayland Smith sat silently, looking neither to the right nor left, but straight ahead at Dr. Fu-Manchu.

"Suppose I decline?" Tony asked hoarsely.

Fu-Manchu struck the small gong. Draperies before one of the several doors were swept aside and Moon Flower came in.

She wore the nurse's uniform in which Tony had recently seen her.

"Yueh Hua!" he gasped and half-stood up.

"Jeanie, darling," Cameron-Gordon's voice rose on a note of deep emotion.

She ignored them. Her blue eyes were turned on Dr. Fu-Manchu who did not even glance in her direction.

"You are happy in your new work?" he asked.

"I am happy, Master."

"You may go."

Moon Flower turned and automatically walked out through the opening by which she had come in.

Cameron-Gordon and Tony sprang simultaneously to their feet. Nayland Smith reached out to the right and left and grabbed an arm of each in a powerful grip.

"Sit down!" he snapped. "Don't act like bloody fools."

Tony conquered the furious rage which had swept his sanity aside, and sat down. Cameron-Gordon resisted awhile, but finally sank back into his chair. "You damn monster!" he muttered. "Why didn't I strangle you long ago?"

Fu-Manchu, who had remained impassive, replied in an undertone like a snake's hiss, "Probably out of consideration for your daughter, Doctor. I am obliged to you, Sir Denis. If you will glance behind you, I think you will realize how childish any display of force would have been."

Tony turned in a flash.

Four stockily built Burmese, armed with long knives, stood behind their chairs.

Fu-Manchu spoke three guttural words, not in English, and

Tony knew, although he heard no sound, that the four bodyguards had retired.

"Now let us hear," Nayland Smith spoke crisply, "what plans for our welfare you have in mind if your generous offer is declined."

His irony ruffled Dr. Fu-Manchu no more than Cameron-Gordon's violence had done. Resting his elbows on the desk, he pressed the tips of his long fingers together. Moon Flower's evident submission to the will of the perverted genius had shaken Tony so badly that his brain seemed numbed.

Waiting for Fu-Manchu's next words, he felt like a criminal awaiting sentence.

"There was a time, Sir Denis," he heard the cool voice saying, "when I employed medieval methods. You may recall the Wire Jacket and the Seven Gates of Wisdom?"

Tony looked aside at Nayland Smith, noted a tightening of the jaw muscles, and knew that he had clenched his teeth.

"Quite clearly," he replied calmly. "Hungry rats featured in the Seven Gates, I remember."

"I have abandoned such crudities. Doubtless they were appropriate in dealing with river pirates, if only as a warning to other low-class criminals. But I recognized that they were useless to me. I had to deal with enemies on a higher social and intellectual plane. Therefore, more subtle means were indicated."

"Go on," Nayland Smith said irritably. "What do you propose to do with us?"

"I hope to make you understand that it is my methods and not my ideals against which you have fought, without notable success, for many years. In England, I agree, those methods were unusual. In consequence, your Scotland Yard branded me as a common criminal. My political aims were described as 'The Yellow Peril'."

Fu-Manchu's strange voice had increased in volume, had become guttural. He had altered his passive pose. Lean hands lay clenched upon the desk before him.

"Was Scotland Yard wrong?" Nayland Smith asked, coolly.

Fu-Manchu got halfway out of his chair, then dropped back into it.

"Sometimes your persistent and insufferable misunderstanding rouses my anger. This is bad—for both of us. You are perfectly well aware that the Si-Fan is international. Ridding China of Communism is one of its objectives, yes. But ridding *the world* of this Russian pestilence is its main purpose. In this purpose do we, or do we not, stand on common ground?"

Tony almost held his breath. He sensed a storm brewing between these two strong personalities. If it broke, God help all of them!

"As I am still employed by the British government," Nayland Smith answered calmly, "your question is difficult for me to answer."

"The British government," Fu-Manchu hissed. "Why do they soil their hands by contact with the offal that pose as lords of China? Can you conceivably believe, knowing the history of my people, that these unclean creatures can retain their hold upon China, my China? Do you believe that the proud Poles, the hot-blooded Hungarians, the stiff-necked Germans, will bend the knee to the childish nonsense of Marx and Lenin? You asked me what I proposed to do with you. Here is my answer: Work with me, for we labor in a common cause— not against me."

There was an interruption; a faint bell-note. Dr. Fu-Manchu stooped to a cabinet beside him. A muffled voice spoke. The voice ceased. Fu-Manchu pressed a switch and lay back in his chair, impassive again.

"Well, Sir Denis?" he prompted softly.

SAX ROHMER

"Unofficially," Nayland Smith spoke slowly, as if weighing every word, "there might be certain advantages. I should be glad to see China rid of the Communist yoke."

"For which reason, perhaps—and unofficially—you had André Skobolov intercepted in Niu-fo-tu?"

Tony suppressed a groan. Fu-Manchu knew, as Nayland Smith suspected, that he had been seen in Niu-fo-tu.

"André Skobolov?" Nayland Smith murmured. "The name is familiar. A Kremlin agent? But I never met him, nor even saw him."

Fu-Manchu bent forward. The hypnotic eyes were turned on Tony.

"But *you* met him, Captain McKay, in Niu-fo-tu."

Tony thought hard, and quickly; tried to act on Nayland Smith's lead. "I was in Niu-fo-tu for less than half an hour—on the run from jail. I certainly never saw the man you speak of there, and shouldn't have known him if I had."

"Then for what other purpose were you in Szechuan?"

"For *my* purpose, Dr. Fu-Manchu," Nayland Smith cried out fiercely. "His mission was to confirm my belief that the man known as the Master was yourself."

The overpowering gaze of the green eyes was transferred to Sir Denis. "Then your trusted agent, Sir Denis, who seems to have acquired what he would call 'a girl friend' on his way, safely reached the house of Lao Tse-Mung to report to you?"

"Lao Tse-Mung is an old and honored acquaintance who has offered me hospitality on any occasion when my affairs brought me to this part of China."

"You mean he is an agent of British Intelligence?"

"I mean that he is a patriot, and a gentleman."

There was a brief silence.

"I, also, am a patriot, Sir Denis. What is more, I hope to save not only the Chinese but the peoples of every nation from obliteration. This will be their fate if the insane plans of the Soviet should ever be put into execution. Their latest instrument of destruction is so secret and so dangerous that research on it is being conducted in this remote area of China."

"We are aware of this."

"Indeed?" Fu-Manchu's tone changed slightly. "We are on common ground again. You regard it with deep concern?"

"We do. If—accidentally—this research plant could be destroyed, its loss would be welcome. Germ warfare is too horrible to be permitted, and Dr. von Wehrner, their chief scientist, is the greatest living expert on the subject."

Fu-Manchu's masklike features melted in a cold smile. "You see, Sir Denis, we must work together. I was informed a few minutes ago that Dr. von Wehrner has been recalled to Moscow."

Nayland Smith started, then shook his head. "Collaboration, I fear, is impossible. The end does not justify the means, and you can't win me over with persuasive guile any more than you could with physical torture. So I ask you again, what do you propose to do with us?"

Fu-Manchu lay back in the chair, so that his strange, powerful features became half-masked in shadow. The long hands rested on the desk and a large emerald seal which he wore gleamed and seemed to shoot out sparks of green fire as pointed nails tapped the surface of the desk. He spoke in a low voice.

"I anticipated your reply. Yet I never despair of convincing you one day that your government, and others, must accept me, as they have accepted the puppet regime at Peking. But my power in China hangs upon a silken thread. The Kremlin distrusts me. In spite of my acknowledged scientific eminence, I have never been invited to inspect the Soviet research station. And I have not sought an invitation—because I intend to destroy it."

"In that," said Nayland Smith, "you have my approval. But you have not answered my question."

Fu-Manchu's long fingers resting on the desk became intertwined in a serpentine fashion, and Tony experienced a kind of spiritual chill.

"I shall answer it, Sir Denis," the whisper went on, almost dreamily. "Your death could avail me nothing and might one day be laid at my door with disastrous consequences; for you are no longer a mere Burmese police officer, but an esteemed official of the British Secret Service."

"Therefore?" Nayland Smith prompted.

"Therefore, I shall see to it that you disappear for a time. Dr. Cameron-Gordon will resume his work in my laboratory here, or perhaps in another, elsewhere. His charming daughter I shall keep usefully employed. Concerning Captain McKay, I am undecided."

Tony had been struggling hard to bottle his rising anger, but as Fu-Manchu's voice ceased the cork came out.

"Then I'll decide for you!" he shouted, and sprang to his feet.

Nayland Smith grabbed him and threw him back in his chair. "For God's sake," he snapped, "shut up." Then he continued smoothly, "There is one objection to your plans, Dr. Fu-Manchu."

"From your point of view, no doubt?"

"No. From yours."

"And what is this objection?" Fu-Manchu bent forward, fixing his strange gaze on Sir Denis's face.

"I will explain it only if you give me your word—which I respect—that should you decline to accept what I propose, no coercion of any kind be used upon any of us to force compliance, and I am not to be asked to identify others concerned. We shall remain, as we are now, your prisoners."

Fu-Manchu watched him in silence for some time.

"I give you my word, Sir Denis," he said quietly.

Tony, fists clenched tightly, glanced at Nayland Smith. What was he going to say? What plan has flashed through that resourceful brain? And what was the word of this arch criminal worth?

"Good," Sir Denis said calmly. "I accept it. You said before that I had attempted to intercept the man Skobolov. On the contrary, I was unaware that he was in China, nor did I know what I should have had to gain by such an attempt. But your evident interest in his movements suggests that it was something of great importance."

Dr. Fu-Manchu did not stir; his face remained expressionless. Tony almost held his breath. He knew, now, what Nayland Smith was going to propose.

"By mere chance," Sir Denis went on, speaking calmly and unusually slowly, "a man unknown to McKay appealed to him to help him. He was very ill and apparently in danger. McKay took him on board his boat, and during that night the man died. His body was consigned to the canal. His sole baggage, a large briefcase, McKay brought with him to the meeting place I had appointed."

Fu-Manchu's expression remained impassive. But his long fingers intertwined again. He said nothing.

"From the correspondence in the briefcase, when translated, we learned that the man was André Skobolov. We also learned that he had something in his possession which was of vital interest to the Kremlin. This could only be a bound manuscript, written in Chinese."

And at last Fu-Manchu spoke. "Which was also translated?"

"It could not be deciphered. May I deduce that this manuscript is the reason for your interest in André Skobolov?"

There was a brief silence. Cameron-Gordon had raised his bowed head and was watching Nayland Smith.

"If it were so," Fu-Manchu said smoothly, "in what way could this be an objection to my plans?"

"At the moment, it could be none. In the event of my disappearance it might prove a source of annoyance. The manuscript is in safe keeping, but should I fail to reclaim it within the next few days, it will be dispatched to the British Foreign Office to be decoded."

CHAPTER TWENTY-ONE

In his memories of his mission to Szechuan, memories both bitter and sweet, Tony found the electric silence which followed Nayland Smith's words one of the most vivid. That clash of mental swords, recognition of the fact that the fate of all of them rested upon the combat, had penetrated even Cameron-Gordon's lethargic despair. There were beads of perspiration on his forehead as he watched Dr. Fu-Manchu.

To Tony it appeared that they held all the cards—but only if Fu-Manchu's word was worth anything. No man—not even Nayland Smith—could stand up to Chinese tortures. He was almost afraid to think about the copy of the cipher manuscript which was in the keeping of Lao Tse-Mung, for he believed that Fu-Manchu could read men's minds. And he knew that Sir Denis, although a master of evasion, would never tell an outright lie. He knew that the original was safe with the lama at Niu-fo-tu.

Dr. Fu-Manchu, eyes closed, sat deep in meditation for several agonizing minutes considering the matter.

What was the manuscript for which André Skobolov had given his life?

Tony, in his agitation, found himself grasping Nayland Smith's arm when Dr. Fu-Manchu spoke.

"Where is this cipher document?" he asked in a guttural tone.

"I have your word, Dr. Fu-Manchu, that I am not to be asked to reveal the names of others concerned," Nayland Smith answered coldly.

Fu-Manchu leaned forward, his green eyes staring venomously at Sir Denis.

"You have rejected my offer. You force me to accept yours. Very well. My word is my bond. What are your conditions?"

"That we are all four free to leave and will not be intercepted; that Jean Cameron-Gordon be released from the control you have laid upon her and returned to her father's care; that I be given an official travel permit to recover the document you want; that no attempt is made to trace my journey or destination."

Dr. Fu-Manchu closed his eyes again. "These conditions I accept."

"Then I can start at once?"

"As soon as your travel permit is ready, Sir Denis. Two others must remain until the manuscript is in my hands. Whom do you wish to go with you?"

Nayland Smith hesitated only a moment. "Captain McKay," he said. "But before we leave, Miss Cameron-Gordon must join her father."

"She shall do so. As my guests they shall be safe and comfortable until your return."

"I accept your terms. But you must allow me an hour to confer with my friends before I leave—in a room which is not wired."

"To this also I agree."

* * *

"For heaven's sake, mix me a drink, McKay. Dr. Fu-Manchu and I have struck a strange bargain. You may talk freely. We have his word for it that there'll be no eavesdropping and as I told you recently, I never knew him to lie... He's the blackest villain unhung, but his word is sacred."

"Okay," Tony said, and crossed to the buffet. Cameron-Gordon growled something under his breath.

Although they were unaware of the fact, they had been conducted to the luxurious suite formerly occupied by André Skobolov.

"How I miss my pipe," Nayland Smith muttered. "Well, here's the situation: Fu-Manchu has his own plans for ruling China. He doesn't want those plans disturbed by a sudden, crazy use of germ weapons. As you know, McKay, I found the name of von Wehrner in the Russian correspondence."

He took a sip from the glass which Tony handed him. "This was news for which Military Intelligence would have paid a foreign agent anything he asked. You see, von Wehrner was employed by the Nazis on similar research during the war. M.I. located the germ plant in occupied France. There was a Commando raid, a German plant completely destroyed. Somehow or other they dragged von Wehrner out of the blazing building and brought him back with them. He was interned, and I had several long interviews with him. I found him to be a brilliantly clever man, and when he got to know me better he confided that although he had devoted his skill, day and night, to the secret researches, he abhorred the idea of germ warfare."

"He would have no choice," Cameron-Gordon declared. "I know the method."

"Later on," Sir Denis added, "he confessed that he had repeatedly delayed results. And I think it's a logical deduction that he's doing the same again. Hence his recall."

"But the situation is different," Cameron-Gordon objected. "Maybe he was never a Nazi. But now he's clearly a Communist."

"No more a Communist than you are," Nayland Smith snapped. "At the end of the war I secured his release and he went back to Germany. I heard from him from time to time; then his letters ceased. I had an inquiry started, and after a month or more got a report of the facts. Von Wehrner had been kidnapped one night and rushed over to East Berlin. Never a word from him since."

"You mean he's a prisoner of the Communists, just as I am?"

"The situation is almost identical. But I haven't been idle. In addition to making the plans which led to our present position, I got in touch with von Wehrner. I foresaw the possibility of things going wrong and realized that my cordial relations with von Wehrner might be useful."

"But how the devil did you get in touch with him?" Cameron-Gordon demanded.

"Through our talented friend the lama. He has a contact in the Russian camp who smuggled in one of the phantom radios to von Wehrner."

"And what is von Wehrner prepared to do?"

"This: If I can guarantee his escape from the Soviets, he will guarantee to destroy the plant."

"But Fu-Manchu intends to destroy it."

"And to make a slave of von Wehrner. I mean to move first."

Dr. Fu. Manchu remained in his seat behind the lacquered desk. Old General Huan faced him from his cushioned seat.

"The ancient gods of China are with us, Tsung-Chao."

General Huan seemed to be pondering.

"You agree with me?" Fu-Manchu said softly.

"That the Si-Fan Register should be returned to us by the hand of Nayland Smith certainly seems a miracle, Master. In the possession of the men at the Kremlin, or the British Foreign Office, it would spell disaster."

Fu-Manchu took a pinch of snuff from his silver box. "Its recovery sets me free to move against the Soviet research plant—a plague spot in Szechuan."

General Huan fanned himself, for the night was warm. "It is this project which alarms me," he stated placidly.

Fu-Manchu's voice changed, became harsh. "I recall, when I communicated with you from England, that you advised against it, pointing out that it would result in a flock of Soviet investigators descending upon Szechuan and possibly finding evidence of your part in the disaster."

"I recall the correspondence very well. As a former officer of the old regime, I am not above suspicion. And having escaped one grave danger, it seems to me to be tempting fate to plunge into another."

Fu-Manchu spoke contemptuously. "Always we live on the edge of a volcano. We are accustomed to such conditions. Very well. Here is an opportunity to achieve one of my minor objectives without exposing you or myself to charges of complicity."

General Huan folded his fan. "Your plan, as I recall it, Master, involved the employment of a number of Cold Men?"

"It did."

"As it is well known that these ghastly creatures come from the clinic which you established and which I constructed, surely this fact would expose us both to a charge of complicity?"

Fu-Manchu smiled his icy smile. "By whom will such a charge be made? At night the circumference of the plant is patrolled by a squad of Russian guards. They are easily disposed of. Members of the staff live in the neighboring village. There is a Russian camp about a mile distant. The guard on the plant is relieved at regular intervals. The wire fence enclosing it is electrified."

"I have made it my business, Master, to acquaint myself with the Russian arrangements. I did so on receipt of your letter from London. It is true that only six men and a sergeant guard the place. The sergeant holds the key to the gate. There is a telephone connection between a box at the gate and the Russian headquarters in the camp. Reinforcements could be on hand very quickly."

"We could, first, cut this connection, then, overpower the sergeant."

General Huan bowed slightly. "Professionally, I should have planned the defense otherwise, although I admit that an attempt to seize the research station is not a likely contingency. It is believed, throughout the area, to be devoted to the study of leprosy."

Fu-Manchu laughed. It was harsh, mocking laughter. "The affair will be over long before an alarm reaches the Russian camp."

"And who will direct these Cold Men?"

"Matsukata. Or I may go myself."

"Master! You would be putting your head into a noose."

"Why? The supply truck from the clinic will be standing by. I will say that the *necropolites* have rioted and escaped. This will be our story if our presence is detected. I am there to recapture them. I had anticipated a possible occasion when a number of these might be used, and so had instructed Matsukata to turn one at large from time to time in order to create popular terror of the creatures."

"You believe that the operation can be carried through without rumor of it reaching the Russian camp?"

"Certainly, if no one blunders. Long ladders will be taken, such as those we have used before, in case we fail to find the key to the gate.

Dr. von Wehrner, who lives in the enclosure, will be seized first. He will have the keys of the buildings, or know where to find them."

And in their own luxurious quarters, Nayland Smith was outlining his plans. "You see, the loss of our mystery radio sets ties me badly. I'm glad we left them behind, of course. If found on us, I don't doubt that Fu-Manchu would have put the system controlling them out of order."

"Tell me something," Tony interrupted. "How long have we been here?"

Nayland Smith smiled grimly. "I know how you feel. That filthy, sweet-smelling gas in the insect room! It might have happened a week ago. But it's my guess that it happened at approximately ten o'clock on Wednesday night. That would make it now about three o'clock on Thursday morning. Events have moved quickly, McKay."

"And now tell *me* just one thing," Cameron-Gordon broke in. "Where is Jeanie?"

But before Nayland Smith could reply, the door opened, and Moon Flower came in.

She wore the dress of a working girl with which Tony was familiar. Her father sprang up at a bound and had her in his arms.

"Jeanie, my Jeanie. I didn't think I should ever see you again."

When at last she turned, wet-eyed, "Chi Foh," she whispered. "Sir Denis. I know what a fool I have been. I spoiled all your plans. Try to forgive me."

Nayland Smith grasped both her hands. "Jeanie, my dear, your devotion to your father and your courage outran your discretion. But you have nothing to be ashamed about. Just sit down and tell us all that happened."

It was a simple story. She had followed them, as Sir Denis had suspected, had climbed the bamboo ladder and tried to keep them in sight when they crossed the garden. When she had had a glimpse of her father opening the laboratory door, she'd hid in a clump of bushes to wait for them all to come out again.

"Suddenly," Moon Flower went on, "I heard footsteps. I crouched down in the shrubbery. And I saw Dr. Fu-Manchu walking toward the laboratory! I almost screamed. There was that huge African following behind him and this horrible man—although honestly I don't think I made a sound—like a bloodhound, seemed to scent me. He sprang to the spot where I was hiding and swept me up into his arms, one big, heavy hand over my mouth."

"If ever I have half a chance..." Tony whispered.

"Quiet," Nayland Smith snapped.

"Then," Moon Flower continued, "those awful green eyes of the Master were looking at me. I tried not to see them, but they compelled me to keep my own eyes open." She stopped, sighed, and clutched her father's arm. "I don't remember a thing that happened after that until I woke up in a room somewhere quite near this one. A kind old Chinese woman was telling me that I was all right and that my friends were waiting for me. She brought me to the door."

"Give Jeanie a drink, McKay," Nayland Smith said. "She needs one. Now, to get back to our problem. Without my radio I can get nothing through to the lama and nothing to Lao Tse-Mung. I don't know when von Wehrner is leaving. It's essential that he have all his plans laid before I can help. This means that I have to get back to Chia-Ting."

"When do we start?" Tony asked.

"As soon as transport and our travel permits are available. But Jeanie doesn't know what it's all about. I'm leaving it to you, McKay, to explain to her."

CHAPTER TWENTY-TWO

It was not long after dawn when Tony and Nayland Smith, driving the Buick Tony had seen before, entered the outskirts of Chia-Ting.

"Everybody will be asleep," Tony said. "How do we get in?"

For the hundredth time he glanced back. He couldn't believe that they weren't being followed.

"We shall have to wake poor Mrs. Wu. I think that's her name. You do the talking, McKay. Your Chinese is better than mine. And don't waste your energy looking for a tail. There won't be one."

Nayland Smith parked near the house of the hospitable physician who had given them shelter. The usually busy street was deserted. They walked to the door; relentlessly pressed the bell. At last they heard movements, and the doctor's old housekeeper opened the door. "We are very sorry to disturb you," Tony began. "But—"

The Chinese woman's expressionless features melted into a smile. "I am so glad to see you, Mr. Chi Foh. The doctor has been very anxious. Where is the nice young Miss?"

Tony assured her that the young Miss was very well, and they went in and up to their old quarters. Nayland Smith made a dash to the desk in the living room and took out the two radios they had left there. He strapped one to his wrist, adjusting the tiny dial.

"Calling the lama," he said, and a moment later, "Nayland Smith here. Regret disturbing you so early... Good... Yes, back at your cousin's house. Just one thing. It's urgent. What is the call number of the instrument you got through to von Wehrner?" He grabbed a pencil from the desk; listened and scribbled. "Good. Now I can move. See you later." Then he turned and said, "Good Lord, McKay, get me a drink. There's still something left in the locker."

He found his pipe and pouch where he had left them, and filled and lighted his old briar. Tony opened the closet which they used as a wine cellar.

"Beer or whiskey, Sir Denis?"

"Beer. I'm thirsty." He drank a glass of frothy imported beer. "Now for von Wehrner," he muttered.

Tony watched anxiously while Sir Denis twirled the tiny dial, which had figures only a keen eye could distinguish. There was a nerve-racking interval... and no reply.

Nayland Smith's lean face assumed an expression Tony had never seen there before. "He can't surely have left already!" Sir Denis exclaimed.

Even as he spoke he heard a faint voice.

"Von Wehrner?" Tony whispered.

Nayland Smith nodded, signaled him to come closer to listen.

"Nayland Smith here. Your delay worried me."

"I keep my radio hidden." Von Wehrner spoke English with a German accent. "I was engaged, and so..."

"Everything is ready, von Wehrner. When do you leave?"

"My Russian successor is due tomorrow."

"Then we must act tonight."

"I fear so. Is it possible?"

"Yes," Nayland Smith answered. "It has to be. How long will it take to make your arrangements?"

"I have already installed the necessary equipment in each of the buildings. No one can detect it. I have only to connect them with the powerhouse and make contact, and all will be over."

"From the time you make contact, how long will you have to get clear?"

"It is a simple device which controls the contact. I can set it for no longer than thirty minutes. But this should be enough."

"What time would suit you best? Give me as long as you can."

"Between fifteen minutes after midnight and one a.m. would be best."

"Good enough. Have your radio handy. We must keep in constant touch."

Tony stared at Nayland Smith. "Does this mean that after getting the manuscript from the lama we are not going to rush it to Fu-Manchu?"

Nayland Smith relighted his pipe, which had gone out. "It seems unavoidable to me, if I'm to carry out my promise to von Wehrner."

"But, Sir Denis," Tony blazed, "what will become of Moon Flower and her father if things go wrong?"

Nayland Smith smoked furiously. "That problem has been puzzling me, McKay. But there's a way out. We must drop by here tonight when we return from Niu-fo-tu and leave the thing in your charge. I'll go on to the research station and…"

"Stop! That's plain nonsense, Sir Denis. I won't do it!"

"I was afraid you wouldn't," Nayland Smith remarked dryly.

Tony began to walk up and down in an agitated manner. Then he suddenly spoke out.

"I have an idea," he said. "If you think it's crazy, say so. We shall have to leave the Buick in some place well away from the germ plant. That's clear. Neither of us knows the route there. The doctor has a car, and a driver who possibly does know the way…"

"I rather like your idea," Nayland Smith joined in. "We take the manuscript with us. Having parked the car, we leave our driver with instructions to wait for us for an agreed time, and then to hurry back to the General's house and deliver the package. This means waiting here until our host is awake and his chauffeur reports for duty."

"I think it's worth it, Sir Denis, on both counts."

It was not long before their host, the doctor, whom they rarely saw, knocked on the door and came in. He wore a brown dressing robe over his pyjamas, an outfit which increased his resemblance to his cousin the lama. Like his cousin he spoke perfect English.

"How glad I am to see you, Sir Denis, and you, Captain McKay. Your absence began to disturb me."

Nayland Smith apologized for arousing him so early, and then broached the subject of the driver for their midnight journey. "We should, of course, pay him handsomely for his services. He would be in no danger, and this will see the last of us. You can sleep in peace."

"You may rest assured that Tung will be waiting for you, Sir Denis. He knows the road to Hua-Tzu perfectly. It is a difficult road at night."

Half an hour later they were on their way to Niu-fo-tu.

Nayland Smith knew this route well; so did Tony. They had traveled it recently with the lama. They were stopped only once, at Jung. But their papers, issued by the governor of the province, produced polite bows and instant permission to proceed. Sir Denis drove the Buick as though he were competing in an overland race, and they reached Niu-fo-tu in just under three hours.

He pulled up in sight of the gate.

"I have been thinking, McKay. To visit the lama openly might be dangerous—for the lama. We still wear Chinese dress. But our visit, coming as we do in an automobile, might reach the ears of Fu-Manchu and result in inquiries. You know the way from here to the back entrance. Off you go. I'll call him and tell him to expect you."

"And what are *you* going to do?"

"Tinker with the engine until you come back."

Tony grinned and set out at a fast pace for the path he remembered so well; the path on which he had found the abandoned Ford and been attacked in the dark by Nayland Smith who mistook him for an enemy. He found it easily and turned in off the road.

The Ford had disappeared, as he had expected. He passed the spot and a run of a few hundred yards brought him out in sight of that stretch of wasteland upon which the rear windows of the lama's house looked out. Although no one was in sight, he slowed to a walk as he crossed to the door. It was wide open, and he entered without hesitation and went on to the door of the lama's study.

"Come in, Captain McKay." Dr. Li Wu Chang, the lama, stood up to greet him. "You are indeed welcome."

"It's good to see you again. Sir Denis has told you what I've come for?"

The lama held up a sealed package. "Here is the cipher manuscript. And here"—he indicated a long envelope which lay before him—"is the result of many hours of labor. I have deliberately held it until it was complete."

"What is it?" Tony wanted to know.

"I have broken the cipher, my son, and this is its translation into English."

"Great God," Tony whispered. "That's genius."

"Merely acquired knowledge and perseverance. There is no merit in a special talent unless its exercise is of use to others."

Tony dropped down on a stool and faced the lama who had resumed his seat behind the low table. A faint smell of incense pervaded the air.

"Tell me first, Doctor, what *is* this manuscript?"

"It is a Register of the Order of the Si-Fan, one of the most powerful secret societies in the world. It contains the names of every lodge master in China, some of them men of great influence. It includes the name of the Grand Master, General Huan Tsung-Chao, governor of the province."

Tony's brain was in a whirl.

"What is the matter, Captain McKay?" the gentle voice asked. "I can see that something disturbs you. It may be that I can help you solve the problem."

Tony, without hesitation, told him of Nayland Smith's bargain with Dr. Fu-Manchu. "Sir Denis has such a firm sense of honor," he explained finally, "that if he knows the cipher has been broken, having said that it was undecipherable, I'm uncertain of his reaction."

The lama closed his eyes for a few moments and evidently reflected deeply. Then he spoke again.

"Sir Denis is a throwback to the age of chivalry. Your course is clear. Forget what I have told you. Take this decoding of the manuscript, but produce it only when you are all in safety. I consider the overthrow of the arch criminal called Dr. Fu-Manchu above all subtleties of conscience. If I err, the error is all mine. Go, Captain McKay, for I know time is of vital importance to you."

CHAPTER TWENTY-THREE

Tony was forever looking at his watch. The hours of waiting in the doctor's house at Chia-Ting had been hours of torture. He was so near to Moon Flower, yet so far away; for not mileage but a touch-and-go midnight venture lay between them.

Nayland Smith had called von Wehrner on the secret radio soon after their arrival, but von Wehrner had explained, briefly, that while the technical staff remained he could not safely talk. Now he was free to do so, and Sir Denis, notebook in hand, was riddling him with rapid-fire questions and noting his replies.

They had met Tung who had undertaken to drive them to their dangerous rendezvous. He was a competent-looking lad, not uneducated, who knew little English. He assured them that he knew the road to Hua-Tzu by day or by night.

He was instructed to have the Buick in condition by ten o'clock.

Nayland Smith made a final note and turned to Tony.

"I have the essential facts, McKay. You're all strung up. Take a drink while I make a rough sketch."

Tony mixed a drink, lighted a cigarette, and watched Sir Denis making a pencil sketch on a writing pad.

"I wonder what you're doing," he said, rather irritably.

Nayland Smith looked up, grinned. "You'll be with Jeanie in a few hours, McKay. The symptoms stick out like brass knobs. Simmer down. Come here and let me explain."

Tony crossed and looked down at a crude plan.

"This is the back of the enclosure you saw. Here is the bungalow where von Wehrner lives. Notice that it's a long way from the only gate, but quite near the wire fence. Here, and here"—he indicated two crosses—"are the spots at which sentries are posted at night. They operate on a circulating system. A moves around to B's post, B moves on, and so forth, every hour. They all report, one by one, to the sergeant at the gate. All clear?"

Tony, now absorbed in the job before them, nodded.

Nayland Smith continued, "Have you noticed the weather? It's going to be a cloudy night. The fence, of course, is devastatingly electrified. But von Wehrner will switch the juice off. He'll join us here." He marked a point midway between the two crosses.

"What about the wire fence? Are we taking ladders?"

"Von Wehrner has made his own. Cord, with bamboo rungs. Easily tossed over the fence. Any questions?"

"No—except where do we park the Buick? Beyond the village there's no road I know of. The Russian camp isn't far up the hill and there's a road from the camp to the research station. But even if we could reach it, we don't dare use it."

"Too bad. We shall have to walk there and back."

At ten o'clock they were on their way; Tung at the wheel, Sir Denis and Tony seated behind.

"We can't use our radio until this man's out of the way," Tony whispered.

"I don't intend to do so," Nayland Smith responded. "Have you noticed the weather?"

"Yes. There's a hell of a thunderstorm brewing. We'll probably be drenched."

Nayland Smith was silent; began to charge his pipe.

Tony thought hard. There were many snags to be looked for. If the storm broke, a flash of lightning might reveal them to the sentries. There were many other disastrous possibilities.

As though a dam had burst in the sky, rain crashed down onto the roof of the car. In a white blaze of lightning he saw the road ahead. It led up into the hills and was little more than a goat track which no sane motorist would have fancied even in ideal weather. Now, it had become a raging cataract.

A crash of thunder exploded like a bomb. Tony glanced at Nayland Smith. He was lighting his pipe. The Chinese driver held steadily on his course, axle-deep in water.

"I presume that this car belongs to General Huan, but I don't want it to break down all the same," Sir Denis remarked in his dry way.

The deluge ceased as suddenly as it had begun. The next roar of phantom artillery was further away, the lightning less blinding. The storm was passing eastward. They had crossed the crest of the rocky hill, and Tony, in a moment of illumination, saw a densely wooded valley below.

They descended a road winding through trees, the driver picking his way by the aid of powerful headlights. The road brought them finally to the bank of a running stream, and here the driver suddenly slowed down.

"This is Hua-Tzu, sir. Do you wish me to drive through?"

* * *

Tony and Nayland Smith stepped out on the muddy track. "I think," Tony said, peering around in the gloom, "it might be wiser to park the car right here. The path to the Russian camp starts at the further end of the village street, I remember."

"Good," Nayland Smith said as he glanced at the illuminated dial of his wrist watch and instructed Tony to switch off the headlights. "Park here somewhere"—he spoke Chinese to the driver—"near the roadside, and for your life don't be seen. Here is the parcel you have to deliver to General Huan. Does your watch keep good time?"

"Yes, sir."

"Then you understand—you wait for us until three o'clock. If we're not here by three, you start for the governor's house. For God's sake don't fall asleep!"

"I understand. I shall not fall asleep."

"Now let's find a spot to hide the car."

They explored back up the slope, and Tony found an opening in a plantation of alders wide enough to admit the Buick. Tung brought the car up and backed in.

"Smoke if you like," Sir Denis told him. "But stamp your cigarette out if anybody comes near."

"I understand."

And so they left Tung and moved on.

Not a single light showed in the one straggling street of the riverside village. They reached the path which Tony remembered without meeting anything human or animal, and began to climb the hill toward the Russian camp. Through a rift in the racing clouds the moon peeped out for a few seconds, and Tony saw the group of huts just ahead.

"Here we start roughing it," he said.

They turned left into a tangle of scrub and made a detour around the camp, in which, as in the village, no light was visible. Above the camp, Tony led the way back to the rough road which connected the camp with the research plant. They stayed on the road during darkness, but ducked into cover whenever the moon broke through.

"We must be near the gate now," Tony decided after a while. "Better stick in the rough and work our way left."

In this way, in sudden moonlight, they had their first view of the wired enclosure and of the hut beside the gate. There was a light in the window of the hut. Beyond, they could see the group of buildings.

"I went no further than this," Tony reported. "To get around to the other side we'll have to explore, keeping well out of sight."

"Good enough," Nayland Smith agreed. "Let's hope there's cover all the way."

There was, until the time they sighted the first sentry. He was squatting on the ground, smoking. Just beyond was a patch of coarse grass which offered no cover at all. They had to creep further away from the fence before they found bushes. Kept on their circular course only by rare bursts of moonlight, they passed the third sentry, who was asleep, and Nayland Smith looked at his watch.

"We're there. And it's just twelve o'clock. We have to wait for the sentries to change over." He lay flat.

As they rested there, they heard the sound of a distant whistle from the direction of the gate. Soon there were footsteps, voices. Then one of the guards tramped past and disappeared.

"I wonder if the sergeant ever does a round of inspection," Nayland Smith murmured. "Better wait and make sure."

They waited for some time, but heard and saw nothing. During a spell of moonlight, Tony had a clear view of the upper part of a hut nestling amid bamboos. It stood less than fifty yards from the wire fence.

"I suppose that's where von Wehrner lives, Sir Denis?"

"According to my notes, it is. He described it as roughly midway between two of the points where guards are posted. I'll try to get him, now. When we know he's starting, we must crawl over to the fence and lie in that tangle of long grass and weeds which borders the wire. Come nearer to shield me from the guard to the south of us. I must have light to see the dial."

Tony did so, and Nayland Smith shone a momentary light from a flashlight on the dial of his wrist-radio, then switched it off. Tony crouched close beside him, listening intently.

Presently they heard the faint voice of Dr. von Wehrner. "I'm waiting in the powerhouse, Sir Denis. If you're ready, I'll make the connection, run back to my bungalow and get what I want, then steal through the bamboos to join you."

"Wait until clouds cover the moon," Nayland Smith warned.

"Trust me to be careful."

"Phew!" Nayland Smith breathed. "So far, all according to plan."

Tony experienced a feeling of exultation and tingling apprehension. Storm clouds were sweeping the sky. "Shall we move over, Sir Denis?"

"Yes. Crawl. And lie flat if the moon breaks through." Their dingy-hued Chinese clothes were admirable camouflage, and they crept across into the tangle of undergrowth fringing the fence without difficulty.

They had no sooner reached this cover when, from the direction of the distant gate, came the sound of a choking scream. It broke off suddenly, as if the one who screamed had been swiftly silenced.

"What the devil's that?" Nayland Smith growled.

Whatever it was it had alerted the sentries to their right and left. Two shouts came simultaneously. Then one of the voices shouted alone, and silence fell.

"I wish I knew Russian," Tony muttered.

"So do I," Nayland Smith said. "But it doesn't matter. The men aren't moving. We daren't use a light out here. So I can't call von Wehrner. We can only wait and hope for the best."

They lay there, waiting and listening.

To Tony, keyed up to a high pitch, it seemed that every passing minute was ten times as long. Presently he became conscious of a vague, muffled tumult from somewhere inside the wired enclosure.

"You hear it?" Nayland Smith whispered. "God knows what's going on, but I'm sure it's something we don't want."

Through a break in the clouds, moonlight peeped out for a few fleeting seconds. Tony stared anxiously into the bamboo plantation masking von Wehrner's bungalow, but saw nothing. The muted, indescribable disturbance continued.

Darkness again.

"Sir Denis!" It was a husky whisper.

"Von Wehrner!"

"Move a few yards to your left. I'm throwing a weighted line across. Be quick."

Tony's heart leapt with excitement as they quickly scuffled toward the spot where a shadowy figure now appeared on the other side of the fence. When they reached the spot, they heard von Wehrner's voice.

"Here's the line," he told them. "Catch it and pull."

Some heavy object was thrown over the fence. It almost fell into

Tony's hands. He grabbed it—a bronze paperweight—and pulled on the line to which it was tied. He had the end of a rope ladder in his hands when it struck.

"Stop pulling," von Wehrner said hoarsely. He seemed to be in a state of panic. "You'll break the ladder. Hold it fast. I'm coming over."

"Hurry," Nayland Smith urged softly. "I think the moon's breaking through."

He and Tony hung on to the end of the ladder as von Wehrner mounted on the other side. Astride the top of the fence, he tossed a briefcase into the tangled grass near Tony, and turned and groped for a rung of the ladder. Faint moonlight through the tail of a racing cloud began to dilute the darkness.

"Stand clear."

As they released their hold, von Wehrner dropped beside them.

"Lie flat down," Nayland Smith whispered. "We must chance the ladder."

They were none too soon, for just then the moon burst fully out from a patch of starry sky, and it seemed to Tony that the landscape was drenched in silvery light, that the ladder hanging from the fence must surely be seen.

The next few minutes were among the most nerve-racking of the night. Von Wehrner was gasping. He began to speak in a low, breathless voice.

"I had made the connection in the powerhouse... hurried back to the bungalow. I went in, using a flashlight. On my desk I had left the ladder, carefully rolled, in a black canvas bag, and my briefcase... I heard padding footsteps behind me."

He stopped, listening. They were all listening. That indefinable disturbance continued, but no sound came from the sentries. The moon was becoming veiled again. Nayland Smith passed his flask to von Wehrner, who accepted it gratefully. After he handed it back he began to speak again.

"I had a dreadful sense of chill. Physical. Something *cold* was behind me. You will think I am mad. I picked up an old lancet which lay there. I use it as a pencil sharpener. I turned, and the light of my lamp showed me a gray thing, nearly naked. Its eyes were a dead man's eyes…

"It sprang upon me. It was supernaturally cold. The mouth was open in a hideous grin. I was held in a grip of ice. I plunged the lancet into the grinning mouth and upward through the soft palate. The creature relaxed and I was able to struggle free. For heaven's sake, what *was* it?"

"I know what it was," Nayland Smith remarked grimly. "And it means we have to move—fast! Dark enough now. Crawl after me, Doctor."

As they crept across the open ground to the cover beyond, Tony knew, too, what it was. Fu-Manchu had chosen that night to raid the research station. He understood, at last, the muffled disturbance which filled the night. The place had been taken over by Cold Men—*necropolites.*

They had not reached cover long when there was evidence that the Cold Men were outside as well as inside. A shriek, instantly stifled, came from the direction of the sentry on the south.

"Back the way we came," Nayland Smith spoke between clenched teeth. "And God help us now."

Then began the detour around the plant by which they had come. Von Wehrner had recovered from the horror of an encounter with a Cold Man and they made good going. Once, Tony heard von Wehrner mutter, "There was no hemorrhage." And he knew that he was still thinking about the *necropolite.*

But at last they reached the point where the road from the Russian camp ended before the gate of the enclosure.

"The gate's open," Nayland Smith said. "They must have overpowered the sergeant, and he must have had the key."

Tony found it hard to credit what he saw. Just before a trailing cloud obscured the moon again, a company of gray phantoms became detached from the shadows like floating vapor or evil spirits materializing, and swept into the open gateway.

CHAPTER TWENTY-FOUR

"W hat's this?" Nayland Smith's voice was grim. They had reached the foot of the path, which came out at one end of the village street. The Russian camp lay behind them silent and evidently undisturbed. On a path of scrub near the river bank a truck was parked.

"It wasn't here before," Tony muttered.

"There's probably someone in the cab," Sir Denis muttered. "We shall have to find a way behind the houses. The truck must be waiting for the Cold Men."

They discovered the path they were looking for, and they followed it to a point where a bend made it safe to return to the crooked street. They had just done so and were headed for the spot where Tung awaited them, when something happened which brought them to a sudden halt.

A piercing scream came from the other end of the village.

"Mahmud!... Master! Help! Help!"

The cry was checked in a significant way.

"It was the Japanese, Matsukata," Tony spoke in a hushed voice. "What the devil does it mean?"

"It means," Nayland Smith explained savagely, "that hell's let loose. Matsukata has lost control of the Cold Men. No time to talk. Listen!"

They heard the grating roar of a heavy engine starting.

"It is the big truck," von Wehrner said hoarsely.

"Back into cover!" Sir Denis ordered. "There's just time."

They ran back to the opening between two small houses from which they had just come out, as the heavy vehicle appeared along the street. Tony tried to see the man in the cab, but failed to identify him. And as the truck passed, from its interior came a sort of muffled chant: *"Looma! Looma!"*

Shocked into silence, they saw the vehicle with its load of living-dead demons speeding up the winding road.

All three were listening in tense suspense. But when the sound of the motor died away in the distance their tension relaxed.

"They have passed Tung." Sir Denis sighed with relief. "Come on. This place isn't healthy."

Tung was waiting in the plantation of alders, and Tony felt so relieved that he wanted to cheer.

"A big truck," the man reported, "passed here soon after you left. It has just passed again. Soon after the first time, a small car also went by. It has not returned."

Tung drove the Buick onto the road, and in a short time they were on their way. Their driver did his best on the gradient, for Tony had urged him to hurry. Nayland Smith consulted his watch.

"We made a record coming down, von Wehrner. Just twenty-seven minutes since we picked you up."

"I was delayed joining you. I set the clock for thirty minutes. But those creatures who entered the plant may have…"

His words were drowned in a shattering explosion that shook the solid earth. All four wheels momentarily left the surface, then dropped back with a sickening thud. Storm clouds, still moving overhead, became ruddy as though a setting sun burned under them. Fiery fragments began to fall in the road and on the roof of the car.

"First class show, von Wehrner," Nayland Smith grinned.

"Two things are worrying me," Tony broke in, staring back at the raging inferno which had been the Soviet research centre. "Why did Matsukata yell for Mahmud and the Master? Was Mahmud the driver of the car Tung saw? In that case, Dr. Fu-Manchu was at the plant when we left! The other thing—who's driving the truck and where are they going?"

Sir Denis began to fill his pipe before replying. "I think it's probable that Fu-Manchu may have followed on. These unhappy creatures he has created are very near to jungle beasts. And the jungle becomes strangely disturbed during an electric storm."

"You think," von Wehrner asked, "that these living-dead have gone berserk and overcome their controllers?"

"I do. I think that Dr. Fu-Manchu, tonight, has overreached himself. Hitherto, I suppose, he has used these ghastly zombies for solo performances, such as the affair at Lao Tse-Mung's house, when it has been possible for Matsukata to maintain control. But a party of *necropolites* poses a different problem—particularly in a thunderstorm."

"Then you *do* believe," Tony questioned eagerly, "that Fu-Manchu was there tonight in person?"

"I have said that I think it probable. What is certain is that a party of Cold Men—we don't know how many—has taken charge of the truck and taken Matsukata along with them. I'm worried."

"Where are they going?" Tony asked, blankly.

"That's just what disturbs me."

The drive back was all too long for Tony. Already he was living in the future and paid little attention to a conversation, in low tones, between Sir Denis and von Wehrner. They had carried out their part of the bargain, for they had the cipher manuscript, and if Dr. Fu-Manchu was the man of his word which Nayland Smith believed him to be—they were free.

They could all return to Hong Kong for his wedding.

His pleasant musing had lasted a long time. Von Wehrner had become silent. Nayland Smith's pipe was smoked. The storm clouds had quite disappeared, and in bright moonlight he saw that they had nearly reached the main gate of General Huan's house.

"I was afraid of this," Sir Denis said grimly. "Look!"

The long gray truck stood before the gate.

"God's mercy!" Nayland Smith whispered. "Truly, hell's on the rampage tonight."

The truck driver lay slumped in his cab. He was dead.

"What's happened?" Tony cried out. "We must get into the house!"

"I'm afraid the gate is locked," von Wehrner spoke in a note of despair.

"Wait!"

Nayland Smith was opening the rear door of the truck.

Matsukata lay prone on the floor inside.

"Get him out," Sir Denis called. "Lend a hand, McKay." Together they got the limp body out. "Dr. von Wehrner, this is your job. Tell me, is he alive?"

The German biologist bent over the Japanese, examined him briefly, and nodded.

"They are tough, these Japanese. It is extreme nervous

exhaustion. Is your flask empty, Sir Denis?"

It wasn't. And the doctor went to work to revive Matsukata.

"McKay," Nayland Smith said, supporting the inert body. "There must be some kind of bell, or something, to arouse the gate porter. Tung may know."

But Tung knew of no bell, so he began to rattle the bars and shout.

"Open the gate! Open the gate!"

He was still shouting when a light sprang up in the lodge, and a door was unlocked. An old man looked out, cautiously.

"Quick. Let us in."

"It is Dr. Matsukata," Tony called in Chinese. "We have business with his Excellency."

The ancient porter came to the gate. "Gladly, for the place is taken over by demons!" He peered about, fearfully. "I saw them, leaping over the wall."

He opened the heavy gate almost at the moment that Matsukata revived enough to speak.

"They meant to kill me," he whispered. "They forced the driver to take the truck to the clinic. I was helpless. They can communicate with one another in some way. I knew this. They acted together. They got at the store of *Looma*. They drank it all. Then they forced the driver to come here. I do not know why they compelled me to come. Perhaps to torture me. From the roof of the truck they sprang over into the governor's garden. All of them, like apes. I know no more, except that the Master…"

Matsukata passed out again.

McKay and Tung carried him into the gate lodge. Then Tung drove the car in and the gate was relocked. Dr. von Wehrner volunteered to look after Matsukata, and Tony and Nayland Smith started off toward the house.

Tony saw that every window in the lodge building was lighted.

"What's this?" he muttered.

"My guess is that the Cold Men are inside. Looting." Nayland Smith spoke rapidly. "By the way, hide your radio."

He began to run. So did Tony.

A gong hung on the flower-draped terrace before the main door. Nayland Smith struck it a blow with the butt of his revolver.

Before the vibration had died away, the big, heavy door was thrown open, and a terrifying figure stood before them; a lean, muscular figure of a man wearing a shirt of chain mail, baggy trousers and some kind of metal helmet. He held a heavy sword having a curved blade from which certain stains had been imperfectly removed!

"You are welcome, gentlemen."

It was General Huan Tsung-Chao!

As the door was reclosed, Tony glanced around the lighted lobby with its exquisite tapestries, trophies, and arms, from one of which, he guessed, General Huan had taken his queer equipment. Nayland Smith was staring at the general in an odd way.

"I can assure you, Sir Denis," the old soldier said in his excellent English, "that I have not taken leave of my senses. But my house was invaded some time ago by creatures not of this world. My steward, an excellent and faithful servant, detecting one of them entering through a window, shot him. The thing ignored the wound, sprang on my steward, and strangled him!"

"The Cold Men," Nayland Smith commented. "What did you do?"

"I ordered the resident staff to lock themselves in their quarters, and took the same precautions with my guests, Dr. Cameron-Gordon and his daughter. I locked the door of their apartment."

"Thank God for that!" Tony breathed with relief.

"Some of the creatures," General Huan went on in unruffled calm, "had obtained knives. Hence this." He tapped the shirt of mail. "It was worn by an ancestor many centuries ago. I called for aid from Chia-Ting and was interrupted by one of the gray horrors, who attacked me with a dagger. They are apparently immune to bullets, but I am a saber expert and I struck the thing's head off without difficulty."

Tony recalled with horror the same feat performed by the executioner in the prison yard at Chia-Ting.

"Listen," Nayland Smith snapped.

A faint sound of maniacal laughter sent an icy chill down Tony's spine.

"Some of them are upstairs," General Huan declared. "They move like shadows. I beheaded another in the wine cellar. The creature was pouring a rare Château d'Yquem down his throat. But there are more to be accounted for. This imbecile laughter—"

A stifled shriek checked him.

"Moon Flower!" Tony shouted. "Lead me to her!"

But that strange figure of a medieval Chinese warrior already led the way. Before a door carved in fanciful geometrical designs, he halted and took a key from a pocket in his baggy trousers. He threw the door open.

It was as if he had opened a refrigerator. Through a window with a balcony outside Tony saw the starry sky, and knew immediately how the Cold Men had got in. The room was a scene of crazy disorder. Dr. Cameron-Gordon lay face down by the window.

A *necropolite*—a gray, corpselike figure—was forcing Moon Flower back onto a divan; his lean left arm locked around her. She was past speech, but her feeble moans stung Tony to fighting madness. With his right hand the Cold Man stripped the clothing from her shoulders, pressing his loathsome lips to the soft curves he found.

Tony leapt forward and pumped three bullets into the Cold Man's sinewy gray shoulder. The creature uttered no cry of pain, but its left arm relaxed and then fell limply. Moon Flower staggered back, collapsing on the cushioned divan.

As Nayland Smith sprang forward, the Cold Man turned, a murderous grin on its face.

"Oblige me by stepping aside, gentlemen," General Huan cried in a tone of command.

Both twisted around, astounded by the words and the manner.

General Huan thrust himself before them. The *necropolite* plucked a knife from his loincloth. And at that same moment the long, curved blade of the great sword whistled through the air—and the grinning head rolled on the rug-covered floor. The trunk collapsed slowly, then slumped over.

"See," General Huan held up the blade. "No more blood than if one carved a fish. The creatures are not human."

Cameron-Gordon had been stunned by a blow on his skull from the Cold Man who had silently entered through the window. Tony knelt beside the divan whispering soothing words to Moon Flower. Her experience with a *necropolite* had brought her to the verge of hysteria, a feminine weakness which she despised.

The icy remains of her attacker, in two parts, had been removed before she recovered from the faint, and General Huan had gone to call those male members of his staff who slept in the servants' annex to assist in the search for the Cold Men still at large.

Assured by Cameron-Gordon that he had suffered no physical injury, Nayland Smith jumped up and glanced quizzically at Tony.

"Come on, McKay," he called. "Jeanie will be all right now with her father. We've got to get downstairs."

"Close those shutters," Tony called to Cameron-Gordon as he started, "and lock the door after us."

Their assistance proved to be unnecessary, however. Matsukata, fully restored, and Dr. von Wehrner, on their way to the house, had almost stumbled over several Cold Men lying in a state of coma induced by a surfeit of looted food and wine. Another, making his exit in the same way from an upstairs window, had fallen on his head and lay unconscious on a tiled path.

Matsukata's manner was furtive. From the way in which he glanced at von Wehrner, Tony knew that there were questions he wanted to ask, and from the way he avoided meeting Nayland Smith's eyes, that there were inquiries he didn't want to answer. In fact, he seemed to be half dazed.

In the light of early morning, Nayland Smith and Tony sat in Huan Tsung-Chao's study, the room with the large lacquered desk. General Huan was seated behind the desk.

"Isn't it remarkable, General," Sir Denis asked, "that Dr. Fu-Manchu should have chosen last night for an attempt on the Soviet station? I had supposed the return of the manuscript before you to be of paramount interest." General Huan rested his hand on the parchment-bound Si-Fan Register.

"It is of great interest to me, also, Sir Denis. But the Master accepted your word that it would be restored as you accepted his that you and your friends should be free to leave. His reason for moving last night was that he feared the replacement of Dr. von Wehrner might result in more stringent precautions being taken."

"You tell me you have no news of him. This I don't understand."

The lined, remarkable old face relaxed in a smile.

"There are many things, Sir Denis, concerning your own part in the affair which I do not understand. The Cold Men, in three parties, were instructed, hypnotically, to obey Mahmud—a former sergeant-major of the French-Algerian infantry. Contrary to my advice, the Master—aware that these awful creatures are strangely affected by electric storms—set out shortly after Dr. Matsukata and Mahmud to take personal charge."

He paused, and very deliberately took a pinch of snuff.

"Dr. Matsukata tells me that the third party, whom he held in reserve, revolted. You are aware of what occurred later. You have scrupulously carried out your undertaking, Sir Denis, and I have arranged suitable transport for all of you, as the Master authorized me to do. I have included Dr. von Wehrner, whose presence in your party is one of the things I do not understand." He smiled again, a sly smile. "If you should call at Lung Chang, please give my best wishes to a mutual friend there. You will be provided with papers ensuring your free passage."

Many hours later, in Lao Tse-Mung's library, a setting sun gleamed on the many bound volumes, cabinets, and rare porcelain. Moon Flower was curled up on a cushioned settee; Tony's glance lingered on her adoringly. Their courteous host had personally conducted his old friend, Cameron-Gordon, and the unexpected guest, von Wehrner, to their apartments, and Nayland Smith lay back in a big rest chair, relighting his pipe and looking gloriously at ease.

"Is it possible, Sir Denis, that Dr. Fu-Manchu is dead?" Tony asked suddenly.

Nayland Smith looked up at him, match in hand. "Judging from long experience, highly improbable."

"Because, it would be rather a pity, in view of something I have here." He pulled out the long envelope containing the translation of the cipher manuscript. "The lama advised me not to show it to you until we were out of danger."

"What the devil is it?" Sir Denis questioned, and took the envelope from Tony.

"It's the lama's deciphering of the manuscript."

"*What!*" Nayland Smith blew the match out in the nick of time, leapt to his feet. "This is incredible."

"A list, the lama told me, of every Si-Fan lodge master in China—some of them prominent persons—including General Huan!"

Nayland Smith dropped back in his chair.

"I said, McKay, when you recovered the thing from André Skobolov, that I believed it to be the most powerful weapon against Fu-Manchu which I ever held in my hands. An understatement. It will shatter his dream empire!"

ABOUT THE AUTHOR

Sax Rohmer was born Arthur Henry Ward in 1883, in Birmingham, England, adding "Sarsfield" to his name in 1901. He was four years old when Sherlock Holmes appeared in print, five when the Jack the Ripper murders began, and sixteen when H.G. Wells' Martians invaded.

Initially pursuing a career as a civil servant, he turned to writing as a journalist, poet, comedy sketch writer, and songwriter in British music halls. At age 20 he submitted the short story "The Mysterious Mummy" to *Pearson's* magazine and "The Leopard-Couch" to *Chamber's Journal*. Both were published under the byline "A. Sarsfield Ward."

Ward's Bohemian associates Cumper, Bailey, and Dodgson gave him the nickname "Digger," which he used as his byline on several serialized stories. Then, in 1908, the song "Bang Went the Chance of a Lifetime" appeared under the byline "Sax Rohmer." Becoming immersed in theosophy, alchemy, and mysticism, Ward decided the name was appropriate to his writing, so when "The Zayat Kiss" first appeared in *The Story-Teller* magazine in October 1912, it was credited to Sax Rohmer.

That was the first story featuring Fu-Manchu, and the first portion of the novel *The Mystery of Dr. Fu-Manchu*. Novels such as *The Yellow Claw*, *Tales of Secret Egypt*, *Dope*, *The Dream Detective*, *The Green Eyes of Bast*, and *Tales of Chinatown* made Rohmer one of the most successful novelists of the 1920s and 1930s.

There are fourteen Fu-Manchu novels, and the character has been featured in radio, television, comic strips, and comic books. He first appeared in film in 1923, and has been portrayed by such actors as Boris Karloff, Christopher Lee, John Carradine, Peter Sellers, and Nicolas Cage.

Rohmer died in 1959, a victim of an outbreak of the type A influenza known as the Asian flu.

APPRECIATING DR. FU-MANCHU

BY LESLIE S. KLINGER

The "yellow peril"—that stereotypical threat of Asian conquest—seized the public imagination in the late nineteenth century, in political diatribes and in fiction. While several authors exploited this fear, the work of Arthur Henry Sarsfield Ward, better known as Sax Rohmer, stood out.

Dr. Fu-Manchu was born in Rohmer's short story "The Zayat Kiss," which first appeared in a British magazine in 1912. Nine more stories quickly appeared and, in 1913, the tales were collected as *The Mystery of Dr. Fu-Manchu* (*The Insidious Dr. Fu-Manchu* in America). The Doctor appeared in two more series before the end of the Great War, collected as *The Devil Doctor* (*The Return of Dr. Fu-Manchu*) and *The Si-Fan Mysteries* (*The Hand of Fu-Manchu*).

After a fourteen-year absence, the Doctor reappeared in 1931, in *The Daughter of Fu-Manchu*. There were nine more novels, continuing until Rohmer's death in 1959, when *Emperor Fu-Manchu* was published. Four stories, which had previously appeared only in magazines, were published in 1973 as *The Wrath of Fu-Manchu*.

The Fu-Manchu stories also have been the basis of numerous

motion pictures, most famously the 1932 MGM film *The Mask of Fu Manchu*, featuring Boris Karloff as the Doctor.

In the early stories, Fu-Manchu and his cohorts are the "yellow menace," whose aim is to establish domination of the Asian races. In the 1930s Fu-Manchu foments political dissension among the working classes. By the 1940s, as the wars in Europe and Asia threaten terrible destruction, Fu-Manchu works to depose other world leaders and defeat the Communists in Russia and China.

Rohmer undoubtedly read the works of Conan Doyle, and there is a strong resemblance between Nayland Smith and Holmes. There are also marked parallels between the four doctors, Petrie and Watson as the narrator-comrades, and Dr. Fu-Manchu and Professor Moriarty as the arch-villains.

The emphasis is on fast-paced action set in exotic locations, evocatively described in luxuriant detail, with countless thrills occurring to the unrelenting ticking of a tightly wound clock. Strong romantic elements and sensually described, sexually attractive women appear throughout the tales, but ultimately it is the *fantastic* nature of the adventures that appeal.

This is the continuing appeal of Dr. Fu-Manchu, for despite his occasional tactic of alliance with the West, he unrelentingly pursued his own agenda of world domination. In the long run, Rohmer's depiction of Fu-Manchu rose above the fears and prejudices that may have created him to become a picture of a timeless and implacable creature of menace.

A complete version of this essay can be found in *The Mystery of Dr. Fu-Manchu*, also available from Titan Books.